ENCOUNTER WITH AN ALIEN

DR. ASHOK SAXENA

INDIA • SINGAPORE • MALAYSIA

Copyright © Dr. Ashok Saxena 2024
All Rights Reserved.

ISBN 979-8-89588-377-8

This book has been published with all efforts taken to make the material error-free after the consent of the author. However, the author and the publisher do not assume and hereby disclaim any liability to any party for any loss, damage, or disruption caused by errors or omissions, whether such errors or omissions result from negligence, accident, or any other cause.

While every effort has been made to avoid any mistake or omission, this publication is being sold on the condition and understanding that neither the author nor the publishers or printers would be liable in any manner to any person by reason of any mistake or omission in this publication or for any action taken or omitted to be taken or advice rendered or accepted on the basis of this work. For any defect in printing or binding the publishers will be liable only to replace the defective copy by another copy of this work then available.

CONTENTS

PREFACE

This science-fiction story delves into the concepts of the soul, death, rebirth, and our working god (the omnipresent matrix) as explained by an alien. The novel covers how I met the alien, how her soul was shifted from the Alps to India, and how her body was reconstructed.

All aspects of physics discussed in the book are peer reviewed, but yet not in the public sphere.

Science fiction, imagination within a scientific framework, opens the door to new possibilities.

It is for everyone with a curious mind and an appetite for true knowledge.

The book aims to answer four basic questions.

1. Who am I?
2. Where am I?
3. What is my purpose?
4. Are we alone in the universe?

The following is the introductory speech of the alien, addressed to the human race and tele-transmitted to me via her helmet, on the 30th of July 2013, in an ice crater in the Alps.

"I am Grengi 137. I am here on behalf of my star's council to disclose to you, Earthlings, that according to the order of the Master of our galaxy, human civilization has been allotted to us, subject to our control. We are conducting various experiments on Earth.

For instance, at the Bermuda Triangle, our ongoing experiment for the past couple of centuries has been to learn how to transfer large objects, such as airplanes and ships, from our universe to a parallel universe. As a result, we have inadvertently transferred some species, including humans, animals, and microorganisms found on Earth. You may occasionally sense our presence or observe remnants of our previous experiments.

Our main goal is to use selected brains to impart knowledge, as directed by the Master of the galaxy. This is part of our mission to educate every resident of the galaxy. This work builds upon our previous experiments conducted by many past generations to pass knowledge to Earthlings. Back then, we simply influenced the thoughts of a few sages or rishis during their meditation, around 8000 years ago, to share the knowledge we had at that time, and it is described in the four books – the Vedas – as a result of our previous experiments.

Our experiments may affect your civilization in other ways. In rare cases, we have introduced micro-alien material into your environment for study purposes, and in other cases, we have removed some harmful substances.

As part of our ongoing experiment to transfer knowledge, we chose a highly optimistic doctor, Ashok, as our subject. We have silently manipulated his brain to guide him in all his research, all aimed at benefiting the masses.

With our invisible help, in 1975, young Ashok conducted pioneering work, **relating biological growth in nature to negative potentials.** His thesis deals with treating twenty cases of delayed union of long bones in human beings using electrical stimulation to create artificial negative potentials for bone growth. This work became the first series in the world and was later included in the *Yearbook of Orthopaedics* in 1979, as well as in national and international journals. Through his research, he explored the possibility of naturally regrowing damaged or lost body organs or limbs by artificially generating negative potentials.

We have been using this principle for a long time, but at a much more advanced stage, with sophisticated infrastructure, to repair damaged organs and regrow accidentally severed limbs. All growing things in nature require and are seen to have negative potentials in growing parts, be it leaves of plants, the cut tails of salamanders, or broken bones.

Similarly, in 1995, after observing the total solar eclipse in India, Ashok could identify the **real cause of sporadic permanent blindness in unlucky TSE viewers who did not use protective spectacles.** He introduced a new theory about 'charged-particle showers' from the magnetosphere through the 'ecliptic window' formed in the shadow area of the moon, based on some crude experiments done at Fatehpur Shikari in the totality zone of the TSE. According to his theory, these showers are responsible for irreversible blindness in unprotected viewers during total solar eclipses, and they also explain all eclipse-related phenomena observed on Earth.

He first presented this topic at the Indian Institute of Astrophysics, Bengaluru, in February 1996, and later in Chung Li, Taiwan, in May 1996. In his first book, *'Inside a Wave'*, published in 2005, he suggested its future application in creating artificial showers of charged particles from the Van Allen Belts (by placing kilometres of large superconducting magnetic loops in this highly concentrated area to further concentrate and focus charge particles), **to generate power** on satellites placed in geostationary orbit, and then transmit it via W.P.T. (wireless power transmission) or electron lasers to Earth, or to other orbiting satellites and planes flying with electric power.

In our upcoming discussions about the soul, rebirth, and the matrix—our working God—we will introduce how and why the Creator used simple physics, which can be called 'Alien Physics' as it is still unknown to Earthlings. I will explain how all physics and astrophysics are based on different expressions of the same space matrix, the continuum of space-time-energy, which is the omnipresent chromodynamic energy of the universe—our working God.

This time, however, the knowledge we have imparted is advanced but simplified. The information will be explained so clearly that anyone with basic school education can understand it. Working with Ashok as a medium, we have shared this knowledge for the benefit of humanity, as it is something everyone should know before they die."

Footnote 1 – Ashok had a vision of using superconducting wire loops tied to geostationary satellites as magnetic lenses to concentrate and focus charged particles from the concentrated areas of the magnetosphere for energy generation (Ref BIB.7). He further suggested that WPT technology, already being used for power distribution in a few cities in New Zealand, or similar technology using electron lasers, could recharge low-orbiting satellites and power fuel-less electric airplanes directly from power stations in the future. In nature, we see strong electric interactions between Jupiter and its natural satellite Io.

Chapter 1

I FOUND MY FATHER DEAD

My name is Ashwarya, and I have been living in Agra with my family and my father, Doctor Ashok. Since 1996, he occupied a hall and a room on the second floor of our house, where he continued his research.

August 15, 2013, was an unusual day. We were watching the ceremonies celebrating Indian Independence Day on TV. My father hadn't come down for breakfast that morning. So, I went upstairs and was shocked to find him pulseless, sitting at his computer with a strange helmet on his head.

In my grief, I sat down beside him and reflected on his life. He was a skilled orthopaedic surgeon with diverse interests, having served as a well-regarded doctor in a government medical institute. In addition to his medical career, he was a productive individual who oversaw the construction of several residential houses, painted, wrote poems, read physics and mythology, and dedicated himself to understanding the fundamentals of creation. He was also keenly observant of human behaviour and travelled extensively.

I noticed his computer was still on, with some text on the screen. There were instructions he had typed for me to follow.

Chapter 2

WE ARE SOUL, WE HAVE A BODY

(A) Crucial instructions on the computer screen

After transcribing this account, I will sit in this chair in front of my computer desk until I become lifeless. However, I assure you all that this does not mean I will be dead, but that I will enter a state called "suspended animation." This is because my soul will be extracted from my body and transported in a transparent jar, trapped in an electromagnetic field by an extraterrestrial being from its spaceship. The spaceship is scheduled to land at precisely 3:58:56 AM local time on 15th August 2013, at the Air Force para-jumping grounds in Malpura, Agra (27.1583144 E latitude, 77.9627741 N longitude).

To avoid attracting attention, the alien has created a camouflage enclosure using laser screen technology, blending it seamlessly with the surrounding landscape. The spaceship will land within this enclosure for a brief two-minute window, and the area will be concealed by translucent laser walls until the spaceship takes off. I left the alien hidden in the green bushes in Malpura, Agra, and returned to my house in my car to document this crucial page.

It is essential that my body remains undisturbed for the next three weeks and is not cremated prematurely. This minimum period is necessary for the journey of the spacecraft to the alien planet.

My alien companion and I have been anxiously awaiting permission from the alien government to transport a living human from Earth to their planet. This unprecedented request has sparked ethical, mythological, medical, environmental, and social debates within alien society. While waiting for permission, we had to act swiftly due to the imminent arrival of the rescue spaceship and the extended stay of the alien on Earth, which could risk her detection. As a consolation, the alien council has granted last-minute permission for only my soul to be transported on the alien spacecraft. However, final permission from the "masters of the galaxy" is still pending and has faced objections from the leader of the opposition in their senate.

Once the alien spacecraft arrives, equipped with advanced instruments, my soul will be tele-extracted from my chair in this room and stored on the spacecraft. It will be enclosed within an electromagnetic field inside a jar for safe transportation to the alien planet. After reaching the alien planet and obtaining full permission from the masters of the galaxy, my body will be reconstructed over my soul using 3D imaging data previously captured by the alien and stored in her "Matrix Halo Camera," along with locally sourced subatomic particles on the alien planet. Although there is significant uncertainty, I have agreed to this once-in-a-lifetime opportunity as it offers the chance to extend my lifespan when only a little time remains. The unique gravitational field and time dilation properties of the alien world promise an extended lifespan on the host planet by possibly 900 years or more. I hereby declare that if my lifeless physical body remains unchanged even after these crucial twenty-one days, it can be assumed that permission to enter the alien planet has been denied. In such an event, I may or may not return to my body, considering logistical challenges and unwanted attention from the media upon my return to Earth. If I do not come back to my body after the completion of this period, I grant my son, Ashwarya, permission to cremate my body according to Hindu traditions on 5th September 2013.

During this period, my body will be preserved and sustained by the imparted energy and a few electrons remaining in my brain from my original soul beam, effectively putting me in a state of "suspended animation." The alien has assured me that my body will be preserved for 21 days, as they have successfully preserved other bodies earlier on Earth without mummification.

The discussions I had with the alien about the mind of the creator and the fundamental principles of the universe in the last 10 days have been compiled daily and are already stored in the computer. A printed version may possibly be beneath some papers in the printer tray.

After completing the instructions, I signalled through the helmet still on my head that I give full consent to her to extract my soul once she enters the spacecraft and to carry it with her, later to reconstruct me on her planet.

Chapter 3

THE PAPERS IN THE PRINTER BUCKET

Amit, my unmarried younger son who was pursuing an MBA in finance while juggling job responsibilities, had planned an exciting itinerary for us. It started with a seven-day student exchange programme in Brussels, Belgium, followed by a 12-day Europe tour. Amit invited me, his mother, Surekha (a retired professor and former head of the anaesthesia department), and his brother, Ashwarya, along with his wife, Laxmi, to join him on this adventure.

Our European tour began smoothly when we joined Amit in Amsterdam. On the first day, we marvelled at Madurodam, Holland's miniature world, which featured replicas of famous monuments, world heritages, and intricate working models of highways, trains, airports, and dams. Before embarking on a canal cruise, we visited a cheese factory and a wooden shoe factory, immersing ourselves in Dutch culture. The sight of windmills harnessing the power of the wind and the abundance of cyclists added to the charm of the Netherlands.

On the second day, as we made our way to Brussels, we caught a glimpse of the Atomium, a colossal structure resembling a 165 billion-times enlarged iron crystal. In Brussels, we visited the renowned Manneken Pis, the statue of the world-famous urinating boy, and the majestic Grand Palace in the city square.

We headed to Paris on the third day. We ascended the Eiffel Tower to behold the sprawling cityscape and enjoyed the mesmerizing 'Lido dance show' in the evening.

The fourth day was dedicated to the Euro Disney Park, where we indulged in enchanting attractions, rode many rides and met beloved Disney characters.

On the fifth day, we crossed over to Germany and embarked on a scenic boat cruise along the Rhine, passing ancient forts nestled amidst picturesque landscapes on both sides. This day tour also took us to the heart of the Black Forest, where we marvelled at the world's second-largest cuckoo clock, beheld the awe-inspiring Rhine Falls at Schaffhausen and visited the lion monument, the lion of Lucerne, that commemorates Swiss guards who died during the French revolution and the iconic wooden bridge at Lucerne.

Meeting the alien was an accident

Unfortunately, on the seventh day, tragedy struck, changing the course of my life. After visiting the town of Lauterbrunnen and witnessing hang-gliding enthusiasts, the five of us took a cogwheel mountain train that transported us via the Eiger glacier to the summit of Jungfraujoch, also known as the 'Top of Europe'. The train stopped at two 'ice stations' where we saw statues carved from ice in these man-made ice cave stations. During lunch at an air-conditioned restaurant at the 'top of Europe', beside the start of a glacier slope, we had a great time playing with ice balls.

Despite being 64 years old, I decided to ride an abandoned ice scooter that I found nearby, left by some body after use. Earlier, I wasn't allowed to ride being considered too old by the sports caretaker, but I didn't want to miss out just because I was a senior citizen. I also ignored the operating instructions from the instructor and, unprepared, started sliding down the glacier on the ice scooter. The high altitude and thin air, combined with my compromised asthmatic lungs and history of motion sickness, soon affected my brain. I started hallucinating and blacked out, losing control of the scooter on a steep slope. As I could not apply the brakes in time, I crashed through ramps and a weak wire fence before rolling into a deep ice crater.

When I regained consciousness, I was surprised to find myself uninjured and being observed by a strange creature of green colour. It gently placed me on the ground and pointed at a nearby helmet. I looked around and found I had fallen into an ice crater, about 60 feet deep. The cave had a faint light coming from a thin beam entering the crater. I managed to stand and looked at the totally green creature, which had a big green oblong shape in place of head, with two long arms and two small legs, but no other discernible features. It didn't have a regular face – no eyes, no ears, no nose, no mouth, no shoulders and no hips. I put on the helmet and the creature started communicating with me through the helmet's built-in language synthesizer, speaking perfect English. Gone were the days of sign language; we could now converse effortlessly, with advanced technology.

I suspected that the alien knew our language from its previous experiments on Earth. I wondered how it could see or hear me, but I realized that I was directly listening and interpreting its thoughts. The alien introduced herself as Grengi 137, a female. She addressed all Earthlings with a speech (quoted in the preface).

Then, she informed me that we were both in a dire emergency. I had fallen into a deep ice crevasse atop Mount Jungfrau in the Alps, with no knowledge of any fellow passengers or the owner of the ice scooter. There was no hope of a rescue team, and I would soon succumb to the freezing temperatures. Grengi had also been left behind by fellow passengers after she accidentally slipped on ice and rolled down a steep slope for a long time, before ending up in this crevasse. After the fall, she remained unconscious for 3 Earth days, with the battery of her communication device loose.

Unable to search for her, her companions had departed, leaving Grengi stranded. She managed to repair the device when she regained consciousness and contacted her home planet to be informed of the situation and request assistance, but they refused to return and rescue her. This was mainly because their vehicle had limited nuclear fuel, only enough for a round-trip journey, and they must have rightly thought about the possibility of running out of nuclear fuel, as the vehicle had already passed the solar system on its way to its mother planet in the last 3 days.

Since then, she had been hiding in this crevasse for the past two days after regaining consciousness. As a backup plan, another spacecraft had already been sent from the creature's mother planet to Earth about 5 days ago. This spacecraft was equipped with advanced searching devices and was dispatched as soon as the creature was declared missing and fellow passengers announced their journey back to the space station at the alien planet. However, it would take around 15 to 18 more days for the spacecraft to arrive, even traveling at emergency speed and breaking the light-speed barrier of the universe, as using all possible modes of space travel. All this was told to me by the alien, Grengi.

Despite her unconventional appearance, I did not fear Grengi; she exuded a sense of grace, calmness, and love. During the past five days in the crevasse, Grengi had been losing strength and growing weaker due to the lack of sunlight, which was her only source of energy.

The alien emphasized the importance of our symbiotic relationship for our mutual safety. She clearly said that I would soon freeze to death and that only with her help I could I save myself. 'And you know the potential chaos that the discovery of an alien on Earth could cause'.

Grengi implored me to take her to my home in India, where she could recharge daily in the sunlight and safely wait for her spaceship in isolation. She was right – I landed here without knowing anybody, and my phone was useless, as I had checked, with no signals in this crevasse. So, it was the only solution for both of us in this do-or-die situation, we like it or not.

Grengi then explained the plan: only her soul would accompany me to my home, leaving her lifeless body behind to be taken care of by microbes. A new body would be reassembled using nuclear debris available locally on my body's 'matrix halo mould'. I was totally baffled, but had no option except to follow her and to execute her plan.

First, Grengi placed her green hands on my forehead, transferring energy to me which also instantly relieved my left knee pain. It was a sensation similar to the cosmic energy transfer experienced during Reiki therapy. My body was revitalized, feeling as if it had gone back 20 years in time. She assured me that this would also protect me from freezing in these minus temperatures.

Then, Grengi handed me a small jar, instructing me not to open it till instructed and to protect her trapped 'soul' inside carefully, after the procedures were completed, and told me that I need not worry about the jerks and temperature differences as the jar would be superimposed with an artificial electromagnetic field. Following Grengi's guidance through the helmet, I turned around and stood still for fifteen minutes while she prepared herself. She disrobed from her strange, transparent-translucent single dress and put a not too big ' halo matrix camera' from her back on the ground. After cleaning and smoothing the ice on the floor and applying a paralysing and anaesthetising medicine all over her body, from a small pouch, she lay still after fixing her halo camera with its three appendages on the ground. Grengi now instructed me to start the halo camera by pushing its button and then to further follow her preloaded instructions recorded for me in the quantum computer inside the helmet for the rest of my journey. The helmet uses artificial intelligence and works with a built-in small nuclear-powered generator.

After approximately 80 minutes, the camera stopped and, as instructed, I collected all of Grengi's belongings, except for her lifeless body, which was left to decompose. I packed the 'halo matrix camera', her strange single dress, a few scrambled pages I found inside her dress, and the jar containing Grengi's soul into my big backpack. I did not forget to collect the empty medicine pouch to be thrown later into a dust bin.

With the helmet already on, with the loaded back pack on my back, I climbed out of the crater. The helmet's computer equipped with a 360-degree camera assisted me in navigating each step of the ascent out of the crater and to the mountaintop restaurant. Before reaching the restaurant, I also stowed the helmet in my backpack and rejoined my group without mentioning the encounter. I managed to avoid drawing attention to the glow on my revitalised body, perhaps the others must have thought it was a temperature effect on my body as I was out in the open so long.

Transporting the alien's soul from Switzerland to my hometown of Agra, India was no easy task. Despite my efforts to be discreet, my backpack now contained several unusual items: a jar loaded with an alien soul with strict instructions not to open it, a 'laser/ neutron beam generator – MRI cum matrix halo camera' with all its attachments, the alien's helmet, and about 30 pages of scrambled text in a strange language, that I had found inside her dress.

Unable to resist my curiosity, and, in an isolated place at night, I finally took a peek into the jar after removing it from its heavy but thin lead metal case, carefully avoiding opening the transparent container inside. I was amazed to see faint beams of light orbiting in elliptical paths, like electrons. It made me wonder about the nature of life and death.

As I reflected on this, memories from the past surfaced. In May 1998, my 67 years old mother, a simple yet intelligent woman, expressed her desire to donate her eyes after her death. I assured her that she wouldn't die anytime soon. Unfortunately, her premonition proved chillingly accurate.

Just two days later, she fell and slipped into a coma from which she never woke up. For forty days, my family, all-doctors, cared for her tirelessly, hoping for signs of improvement.

Even in her unresponsive state, there were moments when we believed she could hear us, as tears welled up in her eyes during our conversations in her room.

On the morning of 27 May 1998, as I sat by her side, holding her hand, I whispered to her that her wish to donate her eyes would be honoured and that if she wanted to go, she could go and shouldn't suffer any longer.

Shortly after, as I began physiotherapy on her lungs with gentle strokes on her back, she suddenly coughed up a large amount of phlegm that choked her. I shouted for help, as the suction machine wouldn't work.

My wife, Surekha, came running but we both could not press the pedal of the manual suction machine, even with all our force. It seemed as if she had been waiting for the assurance that her last wish would be fulfilled before peacefully passing away. After her death, the suction machine was working smoothly. It was a strange occurrence I still can't comprehend why the suction machine failed that day, as a reminder of the mysterious ways in which life works and His instructions are pronounced on us.

Both her corneas were promptly donated to two blind recipients who had been waiting for transplants. Their sight was restored, a testament to the enduring legacy of my mother's selflessness. In the weeks that followed, both recipients visited our home to express their gratitude, serving as a powerful reminder of the impact of acts of kindness, even in times of tragedy.

Foot note: It is ironic that India is home to 25 lakh blind individuals, making up roughly one-third of the world's blind population. What adds to the poignancy is that many of these individuals could regain their sight through corneal transplants, a procedure in which only thin membrane of transparent corneal tissue is recovered for transplantation. What makes the source of these corneas even more remarkable is that they can be donated, from bodies about to be cremated, only with the written consent of close relatives, with or without the consent of the deceased, as law permits.

During our remaining Trans-Europe tour, I sat in the back seat of our bus, which allowed me to conveniently store my large backpack in the empty rear corner seat without inconveniencing anyone. I carried it with me everywhere, even into bathrooms, never leaving it unattended. To avoid drawing attention or receiving unnecessary comments about my large but not too heavy backpack, I made it a habit to board the bus early and be the last to disembark in the evening. I even pretended to be ill during some long-distance sightseeing to avoid any issues. However, I listened to instructions from the quantum computer in my helmet daily secretly in my bathroom at the hotel at night.

After visiting Switzerland, our tour took us to Italy, where we visited iconic landmarks such as the Leaning Tower of Pisa in the Square of Miracles.

In Florence, the capital of Tuscany, we marvelled at the open-air museum of sculptures, which featured statues of royal dignitaries, the renowned scientist, Galileo Galilei, and esteemed artists like Michelangelo and Bernini.

We also explored the ruins of the Colosseum, known for its gladiator fights, and the site of the Circus Maximus, famous for chariot races. We visited the ancient remnant of the Roman Forum, which is the site of excavations of the old city of Rome.

We saw the statue of Neptune God at the Trevi Fountain. Venice, with its intricate network of water channels instead of streets and roads, offered a unique mode of transportation in the city with gondolas.

In Verona, we visited Juliet's balcony, made famous by the love story of Romeo and Juliet, before concluding our 12-day Europe tour at Milan airport on 4th August 2013.

I was specifically instructed to protect the helmet, camera, and glass jar from potential X-ray hazards during security checks by in built computer in helmet. To comply with this, I visualised and before going to airport I searched all day in a taxi in Milan to purchase brand-new replacements: a helmet, a large movie camera, and a glass jar matching the size of the objects in my backpack.

After carefully disposing of the purchased original contents into separate dustbins at different locations and removing tags, I kept only the cartons and receipts. I placed the alien's helmet, halo camera, and glass jar inside the empty cartons of my purchases and then put them all back into my backpack.

When I reached the airport in Milan, I presented my backpack with the open chain to the security officer for inspection and showed them the receipts for the goods. I explained that all three boxes were a bit large to fit into our suitcase as check in baggage and needed to be carried as a handbag. The security personnel carefully inspected the receipts, opened the lids of all three cartons for inspection, peeped inside and found nothing suspicious. They gently returned the cardboard cartons to my backpack without removing any goods out of it or passing them through the X-ray scanner.

Once the aircraft was airborne and we were settled, I retrieved my backpack from the overhead luggage compartment and placed it on an empty seat next to me, to avoid pressure differences. We safely returned to India by long night flight and passed through the green channel at New Delhi airport without undergoing customs checks.

The morning after arriving in Agra by taxi from the Delhi airport, I moved along with my luggage and backpack, into my secluded room on the second floor of my house. The room had a spacious open roof at the back, away from prying eyes. Our tour had been a success, and we had taken a whopping 2,856 photo I transferred them from my camera to our laptops that day.

My immediate task was to help reconstruct the alien body on Earth, with the help of an advanced laboratory at the alien planet, using instruments and technology from that planet.

So, in the early night, after setting the matrix halo camera in an open space at the back of my room and fixing it as instructed by the computer in the helmet, I tele-transmitted the entire 3D matrix mapping data of Grengi's body in the next 4 hours, already stored in its matrix camera, since captured in the ice crater at the top of

Europe. This was required for the formation of the 3-D halo frame of the matrix mould of her body as a rehearsal, at the lab at the alien planet. The same procedure would be repeated later on Earth, in preparation of a 'matrix mould' of the alien body, for the reconstruction of her body the following day.

Chapter 4

DAY 1 – RECONSTRUCTION OF THE ALIEN BODY

(A) 'Matrix mould' to reconstruct the body

What are matrix moulds?

In our sixth class, during our introduction to magnetic fields, our first science experiment was to draw magnetic field lines on a piece of paper using a bar magnet and iron filings. The iron filings arranged themselves into lines which were formed along the layers of the rotating kinetic columns of moving electrons inside, forming the magnetic field of the bar magnet.

It is said that *we should not gaze at stars, but rather look in between*. It is true that we cannot see anything when we look in between because our eyes or senses do not perceive empty space. Space is not empty; space is nothing but a ten-dimensional (10-D) omnipresent matrix comprising three components: SPACE-TIME-ENERGY.

Picture it as an omnipresent multilayered mosquito net, woven systematically by five-dimensional energy particles called **Treo**, with five negative dimensional **Voids** (minute empty spaces).

All *matrix moulds of a body* are formed when a unit space (a cube of the distance light traverses in one second) first contracts one by one in its all 3 dimensions of space (length, breadth and depth) to form 3 types of kinetic coloumns required, similar to the formation of 3 knots one over other in a mosquito net.

The formation of a *magnetic field* occurs when space contracts in two dimensions (visualized as two knots in the mosquito net, one over the other), in length and breadth as invisible two-dimensional shells are formed in the matrix as rotating kinetic columns, due to the motion of electrons in a bar magnet.

Thus, in this experiment of iron foil, we constructed a 2-dimensional mould of the space matrix on the surface of the paper, in which loose iron foils got accommodated according to the structure of this matrix mould of 'magnetic lines of bar magnet'. Now, let me explain some familiar moulds of the space matrix and what they form.

Have you ever wondered why celestial bodies are spherical or why Saturn has rings?

These shapes and formations are a result of the contraction (as wrinkles or knot formation) of the space matrix to form supporting and moulding kinetic columns in response to the applied load of these bodies on matrix.

All celestial bodies are supported by a four-dimensional contraction (four knots one over other) of 'space-Time' in gravitational spheres which forms around their gravitational centres.

As you move away from the centre, in gravitational field of cosmic body, this four-dimensional contraction reduces in one three-dimensional spherical space. This acts as a *spherical matrix self-formed mould*, accumulating mass to construct all celestial bodies in a mould of spherical shape. It is to be reminded that sphere uses minimal area to accommodate any mass.

Saturn is an interesting example. Its rarified mass, with a density lower than water, cannot be fully accommodated in its three-dimensional space pit. Instead, it spills out into two-dimensional elliptical spaces or empty orbits formed in two-dimensional gravitational field of Saturn. These elliptical moulds/ empty orbits are then filled with this spilled out mass of Saturn to form the rings of Saturn, which are formed side by side elliptical orbits of its natural satellites.

Purposeful digging of space matrix is done by growing BIOMASS in its desired shape. In womb the baby grows by filling of desired protein by time bound *digging information* coded in their specific genes. These desired moulds are formed in space matrix by directional and time framed energy transfers by molecules of biomass, with controlled force and with controlled fluctuations of applied degree of momentum (similar to glass blower makes glass objects of desired shape by controlled blow of air from his lungs).

In photosynthesis, controlled energy is transferred by molecules into the surroundings to form a mould in the space matrix of the carbohydrate molecule or the protein molecule and the desired atoms of carbon, hydrogen, oxygen and nitrogen each dock into specifically pre-formed moulds.

The florescence pattern of flowers is maintained by first digging of pre formed moulds in space matrix.

A similar process will be used to reconstruct the alien body by accommodating the nuclear debris (neutrons, protons, and electrons) within the reconstructed 3-dimensional empty mould of the space matrix of her body (you could say that this 3-D matrix halo of her entire body is constructed by the energy channels of her body), which were previously photographed with her matrix halo camera in the ice crater in the Alps to be copied at will.

As it was explained to me, to create a new body using locally available nuclear debris, we would first require one artificially generated three-dimensional mould of the space matrix of her entire body. This mould should perfectly match the deformation of the matrix inside her original body in every minute detail.

(B) **Preparations to reconstruct the body**

The next morning, I loaded my car with various items, including the alien's helmet with quantum computers, the advanced halo camera with in-built laser and neutron beam generators, the electromagnetic field jar covered by lead container containing her soul, my tiffin box, and drinking water. My first task was to commission the creation of a wax model of a beautiful girl weighing exactly 46.81 kilograms, as per the alien's instructions. I found a shop in the Taj Ganj area that could fulfil this request.

Next, I searched for a suitable location to conduct the nuclear process for reassembling the alien's body. I initially explored an abandoned underground chamber in the basement of the historic Agra Fort, built by Emperor Akbar in the sixteenth century.

During my student days, I discovered a gate under the platform of stairs in front of the Shish Mahal building that led to these underground chambers. However, this gate was permanently closed to visitors and workers. A local guide showed me and my late friend, Mr. Bhojraj, this passage and the underground chambers during the daytime. He had the skill to open the locked door by lifting it off its hinges, allowing us to enter silently before replacing the door. Inside, to navigate the sprawling underground chambers, we had to rely on the light shed by a candle held by the guide. Now, I had the light of my newly purchased phone, but the underground rooms and corridors were as foul-smelling as before. The raw and unpolished red stone floors were covered in thick layers of dust and bat droppings. The air carried a pungent and foul odour.

On my previous visit to Agra fort built by emperor Akbar in 16 th century, after we descended three floors, our guide pointed out the male prison and shown us the gallows room. He explained that, after executions, the corpses were dropped into a well directly beneath the gallows. This well was connected to a water-filled trench surrounding the fort from all sides, including under its gates, which used to house crocodiles that fed on the disposed bodies. When we reached the fifth floor below the structure, we entered a large room with mud-covered walls. The guide told us that these walls were the openings of three abandoned sealed tunnels. One of these tunnels joins to Fatehpur Sikri, the capital city of King Akbar located 40 km away built with Agra fort, the second led to Sikandara, Akbar's tomb, built by the emperor himself for future, and the third led to a house building in Agra town, perhaps used by the king for secret nocturnal surveys of city, as mentioned by elders. It's worth noting that the iconic Taj Mahal of Agra was constructed in 17 th century, much later, by Shahjahan, who was King Akbar's grandson, while beautiful monument Etmaduddaula tomb of Mirza Gyas Beg across the Yamuna was built by Akbar's daughter-in-law for her father.

On this particular visit to the underground chambers of the Agra Fort, I ventured alone, carrying my backpack and wearing a

---

FOOTNOTE:

It is crucial not to underestimate the risk of inhaling stale air in the closed chambers for a long time. Decomposing bodies of bats and rats can release harmful pathogens into the air, including viroids (infectious agents that typically infect plants and fungi), viruses, bacteriophages (viruses that consume bacteria), and superbugs that result from decaying wood. These pathogens may have been responsible for the mysterious deaths attributed to the "Curse of the Pharaoh" or "Curse of King Tut." Many of those who opened the chambers in the tomb of Tutankhamun, which had remained undiscovered for more than 3346 years in the Valley of Kings at Luxor, Egypt, died within a year, having contracted strange diseases.

helmet for communication with alien lab at her planet. Through the built-in headphones and camera I realised that someone from an alien planet was also inspecting the building, to see if it suited their requirements.

The alien lab finally deemed the chamber with the sealed tunnels suitable, but later cancelled this site as they were warned by someone about the intense heat generated during the nuclear reconstruction process, which could potentially compromise the fort's structure, built on Earth 450 years ago. As a result, the site was cancelled by me after about an hour as per instructions from the alien planet.

After exploring and rejecting several other locations due to privacy concerns, we ultimately settled on Fatehpur Sikri, where I had previously witnessed a total solar eclipse in October 1995 – an event that had changed the course of my life. Over the past two decades, I had dedicated myself to research in Physics and Astrophysics, sacrificing significant earnings from my private practice and quality time with my family.

To gain entry into the sealed confines of the big open enclosure of Fatehpur Sikri, built by Emperor Akbar (50 kilometers away from Agra fort) at night, I bribed the eight guards of this particular enclosure in the evening with a good amount of cash and a few bottles of imported whisky. I told the guards that I only wanted to take photographs of my fiancée at night, in various poses and at various locations against the background of the various buildings of Fatehpur Sikri. I requested that nobody should be allowed in as I wanted to spend the entire night with my fiancée.

On the way back to Agra to collect my previously ordered wax model, I purchased a burqa. The wax model was ready and I found it resembled a beautiful seated girl. I draped the burqa over the model before placing it in the backseat of my car. Securing the wax model with a seatbelt, I drove the 90 kilometers back to Fatehpur Sikri, arriving there at around 8 PM. The guards opened the gate and waved me in with my car, and I made my way to the gardens deep within the enclosure.

Inside, on a suitable platform in the open, at 9 PM, I activated the matrix camera, which automatically focused and synchronized with the lab on the alien's home planet. For three hours, the camera precisely adjusted its position to account for Earth's motion relative to the motion of the alien planet.

On this still and dark night with no moonlight, under the starry sky, I placed on ground the halo camera with the images of the alien's 3D body that I had taken in the crater, and stored in its memory. The images had been transmitted to the alien planet the previous night.

At midnight, I placed the wax model on the ground with the three appendages of the halo camera around it. The camera had three laser and neutron beam generators, and each got automatically set in 3D at 60 degrees around and approximately 1 meter apart from the wax model. Following the alien's instructions, I set an alarm for 4 AM and rested on a bench in a closed enclosure about 30 meters away.

When I returned at 4 AM, I found the beams deactivated, the surroundings still emitting intense heat, but the platform with the body was cool. I discovered that the alien's body had replaced the wax model.

The process involved constructing an empty 3D matrix frame of the alien's body as a mould, with the joining of multiple copied deformations of the space matrix photos in two dimensions. These empty frames were then filled with locally available nuclear debris from the wax model (neutrons, protons, and electrons) using gamma lasers, electron lasers (technology in experimental phase on Earth), and neutron beams. All produced by the alien's single halo camera, which was being constantly regulated from the lab on her home planet.

I quickly retrieved the glass jar with her soul and her clothes from my car, and placed it near the newly constructed body. Then, after opening the jar, I stepped away to go to the toilet. Upon returning, I saw the alien seated on the floor, clothed in her old attire.

We hastily packed everything into the car, and left at around 5:30 AM.

On the way, via a message from her helmet, the alien told me not to be surprised. She explained that, while her body was newly formed using nucleons and electrons from the wax model, the process was similar to the gradual replacement of tissues in human bodies, grown by consuming the same nucleons and electrons with various foods. Every tissue, including blood and skin, undergoes renewal over time, resulting in a new body on each birthday, replacing the body of the previous year but in the same matrix mould, albeit a bit older and more worn out due to ageing, due to the ongoing expansion of the matrix of the universe.

"We are just a bunch of printed nucleons, arranged on a three-dimensional omnipresent net of space matrix, according to the energy mould of our body details," explained the alien.

Initially, multiple two-dimensional frames (captured by the halo camera, similar to computerized tomography scanned slices while doing a CT scan) are joined together at Planck's least length (minimum possible length) to create a 3D matrix halo of the body as a mould. This mould was then 3D printed using available atomic debris (such as neutrons, protons, and electrons) using laser and neutron beams.

I mentioned that the process you're describing to create a halo of 3D deformation of the body sounds like using streams of channelized energy that precisely copy it in a three-dimensional empty frame. It's something like the process used in television where two-dimensional frames of space matrix deformation/ contraction are transmitted as pieces via a one-dimensional electromagnetic wave of photon beams from a studio camera to be reassembled as 2D pictures on your TV screen.

The reconstruction of whole bodies in artificially formed matrix halo moulds is in experimental phase and new on our planet, and sometimes this reconstruction of bodies is required during our routine many centuries long trans-galactic journeys. We store the bodies of our astronauts in liquid nitrogen. Their soul is extracted and travels in an electromagnetic shield inside lead jars. The astronauts after reaching its destination are reconstructed by pre-programmed robots and brought back to life.

Chapter 5

DAY 2 – ALL ABOUT SOUL

(a) First Day in the Room

I am a curious person. My thirst for knowledge is unending. Out of this curiosity, I have read epics like the Mahabharat and Ramayana, and have explored the Geeta, Bible, and Quran. I have also learned about Buddha, Guru Nanak, Abraham, and Confucius. I have observed nature and human behaviour in depth. I have read numerous books on physics.

Since the day I met the alien, I have been pondering the nature and structure of the soul. As soon as we settled into our room on the second floor of my house in Agra, after having breakfast and the alien spending 5 hours in the sun on the 8th day, around 11:30 AM, I asked the alien if we could discuss the soul.

She replied, "First, tell me what you know about the soul?"

I used to give lectures on the soul, as it was my favourite topic among our small group of friends.

So, I began hastily and said as I always starts, **'You don't have a soul, you are soul, you have a body'.**

"Consciousness about oneself and one's surroundings is a feature of all living beings, it's our governing soul."

In the Shri Bhagavad Geeta, which is part of the epic Mahabharata, the great war of Mahabharat was fought in

3137 BC in Kurukshetra, Haryana, India. Arjun, the great archer, faced a dilemma. He didn't want to harm or kill his relatives and friends, so he decided to put down his bow and arrow in the battle field. Lord Krishna, serving as his chariot driver, then revealed the truth to Arjun about the soul. I found only one literature about the soul.

Lord Krishna, in Sanskrit the Vedic language, explained to Arjun as below

अविनाषि तु तद्विद्धि येन सर्वमिदं ततम् ।

विनाषमव्ययस्यास्य न कष्चित्कर्तुमर्हति । 17 ।

It is imperishable, pervaded everywhere in body and no one can destroy it.

अन्तवन्त इमे देहा नित्यस्योक्ता: षरीरिण: ।

अनाषिनोऽप्रमेयस्य तस्माद्युध्यस्व भारत । 18 ।

Perishable body is immersed with this indestructible.

य एनं वेत्ति हन्तारं यष्चैनं मन्यते हतम् ।

उभौ तौ न विजानीतो नायं हन्ति न हन्यते । 19 ।

Killer cannot kill it, know it is never killed.

न जायते म्रियते या कदाचित्रायं भूत्वा भविता वा न भूय: ।

अजो नित्य: षाश्वतोऽयं पुराणो न हन्यते हन्यमाने षरीरे । 20 ।

Never Born or die ever (past, present or future), unborn, eternal, permanent, oldest, not destructible with destructible body.

व्दविनाषिनं नितयं य एनमजमव्ययम् ।

कथं स पुरुष: पार्थ कंघातयति हन्ति कम् । 21 ।

Know it, indestructible, always existing, unborn, immutable it is, then tell me WHO kills WHOM.

वासांसि जीर्णानि यथा विहाय नवानि गृह्णाति नरोऽपराणि।

तथा षरीराणि विहाय जीर्णान्यन्यानि संयाति नवानि देही । 22 ।

Old clothes are thrown and accepted new one by man, similarly it leaves decayed body to get new body.

चैनं छिन्दन्ति षस्त्राणि नैनं दहति पावकः।

न चैनं कुंदयन्त्यापो न षोशयति मारुतः । 23 ।

Nor divisible with any weapon, nor burnt with fire, not moistened by water, or moved by wind,

अच्छेपोऽयमदाह्योऽयमनुद्योऽषोष्य एव च।

नित्यः सर्वगतः स्थाणुरचलोऽयं सनातनः । 24 ।

Unbreakable, un-burnt, in-soluble, can't be dried certainly ever lasted, present everywhere, unchangeable, immovable and same from eternity.

अव्यक्तोऽयमचिन्त्योऽयमविकार्योऽयमुच्यते।

तस्मादेवं विदित्वैनं नानुषोचितुमर्हसि । 25 ।

Invisible soul, inconceivable soul, un-changeable soul, knowing this don't lament for just body.

अथ चैनं नित्यजातं नित्यं वा मन्यसे मृतम्।

तथापि त्वं महाबाहो नैवं षोचितुमर्हसि । 26 ।

If, however you think it is always born every time and will die every time, even then o mighty lament is not desired.

जातस्य हि ध्रुवो मृत्युर्युर्व जन्म मृतस्य च।

तस्मादपरिहार्येऽर्थे न त्वं षोचितुमर्हसि । 27 ।

One who has taken birth will definitely die therefore for any inevitable, lament is not deserved.

अव्यक्तादीनि भूतानि व्यक्तमध्यानि भारत।

अव्यक्तनिधनान्येव तत्र का परिदेवना । 28 ।

Initially un-manifested, it manifests in middle to become unmanifested again after its inhalation.

आष्चर्यवत्पष्यति कश्चिदेनमाष्चर्यवद्वदति तथैव चान्यः।

आष्चर्यवच्चैनमन्यः श्रृणोति श्रुत्वाप्येनं वेद न चैव कष्चित् । 29 ।

Some see soul amazing; some speaks it amazing; some hear it amazing, but even thereafter cannot understand it.

देही नित्यमवध्योऽयं देहे सर्वस्य भारत।

तस्मात्सर्वाणि भूतानि न त्वं षोचितुमर्हसि । 30 ।

This owner of material body is eternal, so descendent of king Bharat you never lament for body of any living.

After I stopped, then the alien explained to me,

(b) The soul has two divisions and five quantum levels

The soul is divided into two parts: **PRAN ATMA** (the super soul or cosmic consciousness, also known as Vibhu Atma) and **JEEV ATMA** (individual souls).

The Jeev Atma, or individual soul, has five quantum levels, which are distinct from the supreme soul's consciousness, as the Vibhu Atma has complete knowledge of the past, present, and future.

The Svetasvatara Upanishad, dating back to the 4th or 5th century BC, describes the soul as being incredibly small—comparable to a hundredth of the thickness of a hair. This is roughly equivalent to the size of 87 billion electron beam in a human soul. The Sanskrit verse says:

"Balagra-sata-bhagasya, satadha kalpitasya ca, bhago jivah sa vijneyah, sa canantyaya kalpate."

Curious about the claim* that electrons possess a bit of mind, I enquired the alien.

She confirmed that electron infect act as 'bit of soul', and further elaborated,

Atma, soul, mind, consciousness, and life are synonymous and is represented by presence of multiple electron beams in all living beings. The soul needs creation of ten-dimensional space, comprising two predominant five-dimensional energy centres—positive and negative—that act as two common foci for all electrons orbiting in elliptical paths in different plains in our brain or this consciousness is extended in the body of creature along its nervous system, with electrons moving in closed circuits.

The positive energy centre is created by *increasing contraction* of the local space matrix, while the negative energy centre is formed by *increasing dilatation*. These two energy centres serve

---

FOOTNOTE:

Freeman Dyson, in his book Disturbing the Universe (1979), suggested that the **"process of human consciousness is similar to the choices made by electrons, differing only in degree, not in kind".**

as two common foci of orbits of all 87 billion electrons forming the soul's beam in humans.

All electrons circulating in elliptical orbits as a beam, connects the two cerebral cortices of the brain and all are quantum entangled in all living beings. Some of these electrons follow complex paths that form the nervous system, enabling consciousness to spread throughout the body. Sensory information as moving electrons is transmitted as electrical impulses, which travel at 2,200 km per second (the speed of light multiplied by 1/137, the value of fine-structure constant). These energy signals carried by different quanta of electrons (just like different quanta of photons) which allow the brain to process sensations and reactions.

Every thought creates a wrinkle in the space matrix of different lengths, produced by a chain of kinetic coloumns along the wavelength (depends on different quanta of EM energy in packet) of each photon in the beam which are responsible for that particular thought. In this way, electron function like the bit of a computer and are the fundamental unit of consciousness.

(c) Five levels of consciousness

'Kan Chetna' in Atoms of all elements. (1 to 120)

'Jad Chetana' in all plants.

'Pashu Chetna' in all animals.

'Jan Chetna' in all humans. (86 billion electrons)

'Bliss' – attachment with detachment, a happy state.

To delve further into the elliptical orbits of the soul's beam, the progressive contraction of matrix towards the positive energy centre influences **male behaviour** and serves as the dominant characteristic in males of all species.

On the other hand, the progressive relaxation of matrix towards the negative energy centre is responsible for **female characteristics** and behaviour, prevailing in females of all species.

The gender of a soul is determined by the unequal ratio of the contracting Yang and relaxing Yin, two matrix energy fields, which form two common centres for elliptical orbits of all orbiting electrons in beam.

Figure 1 – The unequal ratio of the Yang and Yin fields in the common orbit of the beam of the soul decides the gender of this soul

(d) Difference Between a Living Being and a Dead Body

One way to confirm the death of a living being is to observe a flat line on an electroencephalogram (EEG) or to note the absence of electrical activity in recordings from "brainstorm" tests, which map the brain's electrical conduction. Sensations in the body are relayed to the brain through sensory nerves, and then actions are executed via motor nerves that transmit electrical impulses to produce a response. Consequently, the electrical conduction in the brain and the flow of electric current, which represents the movement of electrons in the nervous system, are fundamental characteristics of all living beings. These electrical activities in the brain and body are absent in a dead organism.

It is important to note that, fundamentally, only quantum-entangled neurons on both sides of the cerebral cortex interact with each other and are responsible for consciousness (soul, life, or mind). Some functions performed by the brain and spinal cord happen instantly, before we can consciously think about them. These are known as "reflex actions"; for example, we blink our eyes without any input from our conscious mind in response to an approaching object. Neurons in the cerebellum are primarily responsible for the functioning of the heart, lungs, and basic instincts, rather than for consciousness, but they are still governed by it. After the cerebral cortex stops functioning and a person is declared "brain dead," the cerebellum may continue to operate, keeping the heart and lungs functioning for a few weeks with life support systems. There is recorded history of a heart working for 56 years while the brain was dead, and the body remained in a coma, sustained by an iron lung machine.

(e) What is the Science behind death?

The beam of the soul moves around two foci in elliptical orbits, one being the kinetic energy centre. As it moves toward this foci, the electrons gain speed; conversely, when moving toward the other foci, the "potential energy centre," or vacant focus, the electrons lose speed. The inhalation of two opposing energy centres by each other releases the "beam of the soul," which, along with all the orbiting electrons around the two foci, results in the death of an organism. Consequently, the flow of all electrons in the brain and nervous system also ceases.

(f) Why Do All Creatures Sleep, and What is Sleep?

She replied, "During sleep, our bodies and souls rearrange themselves. This instinct is similar to the changes occurring between two vibrations; the universe rearranges itself. Thus, as the soul within the body rearranges its deformations during sleep, it can sharpen its previous life memories (i.e., all thoughts manifest as wrinkles in different wavelengths of photons of varying quantum energy), which are carried into the next life, attached to the electron beam of the soul.

Only 10 percent of the brain operates as the conscious brain when we are awake, while 90 percent functions as our subconscious brain. During sleep, as the electrons rearrange, the plane of our consciousness diminishes, and the subconscious brain takes control of the body. That is why, sometimes, when we briefly awaken at night, ideas flash in our minds that have been processed by our subconscious brain over many days. We often receive answers to lingering problems or questions from our subconscious, leading to significant discoveries, such as the molecular structure of benzene, credited to the workings of our subconscious brain. Some scientists even learn to train their brains for this purpose.

FOOTNOTE:

Just as electrons and planets orbit in elliptical paths around the Sun, gaining speed when moving toward the Sun (the kinetic energy centre) and slowing down as they move toward the vacant focus (maximum potential energy), this property of the matrix was described by Kepler in 1609 as his second "Law of Areas."

I almost exclaimed, "I have successfully relied on this aspect of brain function and found answers to many of my questions."

We need the full energy of our body and brain to rearrange the orbits of the electron beams that constitute our soul. This can be achieved by lowering our level of consciousness and stopping many bodily functions, along with all new inputs, such as the functioning of sight and other body systems during sleep. During sleep, the body repairs itself; abnormal and ever-forming cancer cells are destroyed, we combat ailments and illnesses, immunity is boosted, and children grow rapidly. The consciousness or soul, while rearranging itself during sleep, can access its past life memories as deeply buried deformations, which can surface and be grasped by the new brain of a child in this life.

(g) **Conservation of the Soul**

The soul consists of electron beams (responsible for consciousness) and photon beams (representing thoughts), both creating wrinkles in the space matrix (the omnipresent universe). The conservation of the soul is analogous to the conservation of momentum. Just as photon beams create wrinkles in the matrix in one dimension (one knot in the matrix), electron beams cause two-dimensional contractions of space (two knots, one over the other). These deformations, or wrinkles, once formed on the matrix, cannot be erased by themselves and are therefore conserved indefinitely.

Every thought and event leave a permanent mark on the soul, forming new wrinkles that ensure both consciousness and thoughts persist forever unless they dissolve with the matrix. Just as a photon moves indefinitely along a one-dimensional deformation (wrinkle), which only changes hands (can only form new wrinkles in the direction of its motion) but cannot be erased (without counter-deformation), the deformations (wrinkles) of the soul continue to exist indefinitely as a "conservation of soul," which persists through changes in bodies until it dissolves with the matrix—referred to as salvation or "moksha" in Sanskrit.

(h) Tell me about Rebirth?

The undisputed proof of rebirth is the memories of previous life, which are sometimes revealed but always transmitted along with the soul to its next birth.

<u>REBIRTH IN VEDAS</u>

(!) Yajurveda 4 | 15 | |

पुनर्मनः पुनरायुर्मे आ ॑गृन् पुर्नः प्रा.ः पुनरात्मा म॒आन् ।

(जीव पुनःपुनः मन इन्द्रिय प्राण आयु प्राप्ति की इच्छा करता है ।)

"The soul repeatedly seeks to regain mind, senses, life, and age."

(!!) Atharvaveda 11 | 4 | 20 | |

अन्तर्गर्भश्चरति देवतास्वार्भूतो भूतः स उ जायते पुनः ।

(जीव गर्भपिण्ड में गतिमान् होते हुये पुनः पुनः उत्पन्न होता है ।)

"Living beings activated in the womb are born again and again."

(j) Scientific Studies of Rebirth

More than 2,700 confirmed cases of rebirth have been rigorously investigated in North India, revealing credible elements. In all instances, children aged 2 to 6 retained memories of their past lives (Division of Personality Studies, University of Virginia—Stevenson et al., 1961-1974; Cook et al., 1983, and others). These children could recognize individuals and recount events from their past lives, often retaining behavioural traits such as rituals and phobias. Interestingly, there were no cases of gender change or birth from non-human species, suggesting that the number of electrons in the soul beam and the balance of Yin and Yang energy with its unequal ratio, is conserved as such and remains consistent across rebirths.

Out of the 2,700 cases, all souls reincarnated into bodies matching their gender, with one exception: a female soul was reborn in a male body but retained female behaviours and preferences. In some same-sex marriages, it's possible that one partner might possess a soul of the opposite gender. One case even reported a soul remembering its past two lives.

(k) The Soul as the Primary Memory Carrier from One Life to the Next

The soul, represented by the wrinkles formed by the beam of electrons, along with those formed by thoughts and events of life (represented by beams of photons of different wavelengths), is carried into its next life, imprinting the new brain. Sometimes, these imprints sharpen into past life memories while the soul rearranges itself during sleep, allowing the child to share these memories with someone when they awaken.

FOOTNOTE:

1. My 66-year-old friend, Bijendra, continued using the name from his previous life, which he adopted in childhood. At age 3, he told his father, "How can you forget me? I am your uncle, Bijendra."

2. A famous case involved Suresh, a murder victim who owned Suresh Radio Shop in Agra. He was reborn in the same city, bearing a birthmark where he had sustained a bullet wound. The child would say, "I am Suresh," and recount details of his previous life and the circumstances of his death.

3. A male soul in a female body opted for mastectomy (removal of her breasts) as unacceptable alien parts to his male soul, performed secretly by one of my colleagues in Agra.

(I) Salvation (Moksha or Kevalya as Named in the Vedas)

The highest level of consciousness is bliss, where humans exist in a perpetual state of joy. The soul is least attached to the brain and worldly attractions, exhibiting little or no ego. Rishis achieve this state by entering a deep state of samadhi, while we engage in daily meditation to bring our souls closer to this state of bliss.

In this state of bliss, the soul remains unentangled and free from all attachments, functioning with detachment from the world while performing all work as assigned duty. In salvation after death, all formed small wrinkles of electron orbits, when in a state of bliss or incarnation, can easily dissolve into the fabric of the matrix (God) and lose their individuality to attain salvation, also known as moksha or Kevalya in the Vedas.

The soul can achieve moksha immediately after death or, at times, later, once its entangled knots are untied through the fulfilment of remaining desires by someone. Upon attaining salvation (moksha), the soul's deformations or wrinkles on the space matrix, which are otherwise conserved as the "conservation of soul," will disappear. Once the soul becomes a part of the matrix (our working God), and thus, this immortal soul will no longer require rebirth.

If salvation is not attained, the soul after death lives in **sixth level of being**; free in space after death, even for a few years (one soul, studied with rebirth cases, was born after a gap of 17 years, as revealed by 3 years old child, along with the narration of many other correct past life incidences).

(m) Quantum Jump of the Soul to a Higher Quantum Level

Can the soul ascend to higher levels of consciousness?

Yes, the soul can ascend to higher levels of consciousness during life through our actions by gathering more electron beams, ultimately reaching a state of bliss. By nurturing the soul through peace, happiness, and love for nature, and by helping others with **Nishkam Karma** (performing actions as a duty without seeking rewards), one can accumulate electrons. This elevation allows the soul to rise to a higher quantum level of bliss and even strengthen it towards achieving incarnation. At this level of incarnation, one gains mastery over the workings of the matrix and can perceive others' past or future lives.

(n) Can the Soul Descend to Lower Levels of Consciousness?

The soul's quantum level is influenced by negative emotions, excessive desires, ego, cruelty, insensitivity, and excessive attachment to material possessions. These factors result in the soul becoming entangled with the matter of the brain, creating a sort of cage. Even during life, the soul may descend to a lower quantum level, gradually losing its electrons and leading to a form of self-killing consciousness.

However, changes in quantum levels (the number of electrons in its beam) without strong new inputs are rarely observed. In extreme cases, a human soul may descend to an animal soul after the death of a person who lived with animalistic behaviour and showed disrespect towards the creator, creation, and creatures. This descent can also be temporary; the soul can recover by unentangling itself from worldly attachments and freeing itself from the neurons of the brain. By letting go of excessive ego, the soul can regain its former level or even ascend to a higher level of bliss.

The entanglement of the soul with the brain can be deep and extreme, whether due to ego, sexual desires, or love. As the electrons in the soul's beam become heavily entangled with certain parts of the brain, they may not be freed at death. The soul can descend to lower quantum levels, resulting in the partial release of its beam at death, which can then manifest as an animal soul.

Another rare way the soul may descend is by donating some portion of its electron beam to another person during life or after death, often to help or bless that individual, or to fulfil remaining duties through them.

(o) How Can the Soul Be Donated to Another Soul?

She explained, "Have you heard of rishis giving blessings or miraculous occurrences where someone is cured of a life-threatening condition? These are examples of one soul strengthening another. You transfer electrons of universe via Rekhi master as medium in treatments by touch therapy of REKI and mobilizes energy in body by AQUA PRESSURE TECHNIQUES, or Earth this energy via AQUA PUNCTURE.

Two souls, like magnetic fields, can merge to become more powerful and blend together as 'electron beams' of energy. A loved one can even donate, with its strong will, their entire soul to another to strengthen that soul at the time of death.

FOOTNOTE:

Remember Kabir's saying: "When my ego was there, God was not. Now God is there, but my ego has gone. The darkness vanished when the lamp was lit."

(p) Is Our Universe Conscious?

When I asked, "Is our universe conscious?" she responded that this is a debated topic among scientists, even on our planet.

I mentioned that Dirac postulated that the universe is a pool of electrons existing everywhere (in fact, it is the baseline energy of the matrix). Some believe that, similar to bits in a computer, free electrons might possess "a bit of mind" or consciousness. To my knowledge, quantum computers operate by reading anticlockwise cycles of electrons as 1 and clockwise cycles of positrons as 0. While the brain can perform 10^{16} computations per second, the universe operates at a much larger scale, processing 10^{106} computations per second. Despite this vast difference, it remains unclear whether the universe itself is conscious. However, every occurrence in the universe seems to have a purpose, and it functions as a unified entity to fulfil this purpose, even if we may not always understand it.

She said, "I cannot definitively answer whether the universe is conscious. However, I will provide you with knowledge about the complete workings of the universe and its laws. Only then will you appreciate some of its behaviors, which may suggest a 'conscious universe,' allowing you to relate that all purposeful actions in the universe are being performed according to His will."

FOOTNOTE:

There's a documented case where a man struck by lightning, instead of being injured, found that his eyesight and joint pain were miraculously healed (Book of Facts: Reader's Digest). It is possible that the electrons from the lightning he was struck were passed and mixed with the electron beam of his soul, thereby strengthening it.

Chapter 6

DAY 3 – WHO AM I? & WHERE I AM?

(1) Who we are?

Overwhelmed by the previous discussions, a question suddenly came to mind, and I asked the alien.

"The human race has an eternal quest in the form of two unanswered questions. As soon as we are born and open our eyes, we begin searching for 'Where am I?' And 'Who I am?"

Once free from the daily struggles of survival, where we spend our entire lives consumed by the pursuit of food, shelter, and clothing, we sometimes find ourselves scratching our heads and seeking answers from mythological figures, self-proclaimed 'gods,' in hopes of finding the answers to these questions. But in the end, we all die unsatisfied.

In the Katha Upanishad, there is a story where NACHIKETA asked YAM RAJ, the God of death, to answer these questions. Which remains only a story of that time."

(2) We are souls; we have bodies

She replied, "Our bodies exist solely to nourish this cage of our soul, i.e., our brain, which entangles within itself our soul or mind. We have already discussed this mind (synonyms: soul, consciousness, or life). Bodies can be in any form. They can be human or animal,

---

FOOTNOTE:

NACHIKETA is a human character and YAM RAJ is the God of death, from the story in the Katha Upanishad, written in the 5th century AD.

may have beaks like birds, or be like my body, which is more or less like a plant but produces offspring like you.

She replied, "Basically, all bodies, whether microbes, plants, or animals, are made up of proteins, carbohydrates, and fats, which are composed of atoms of different elements. All atoms of all elements are made up of different numbers of neutrons and their counterpart protons, formed after their beta decay, which remains quantum entangled with an accompanying orbiting electron to balance each other's charge. It is important to note that neutrons, protons, and electrons are not point masses, but rather mass-energy packets positioned at specific quantum levels, and they all spread evenly along their wavelengths, which are reciprocal to their total mass while they go on circling in wave motion in their respective orbits. This circular motion creates angular deformations that need to be balanced by counter deformations; that is why two-dimensional (elliptical) whirlpool-like twin deformations in the space matrix are formed at the first four atomic quantum levels. With each increase of positive charge at the nucleus, due to the addition of one proton repeatedly (i.e., increasing atomic number), the new empty elliptical orbits formed are filled one by one with + spin and – spin electrons, both in each solo orbit to form different atoms of all elements.

Thus, based on the difference in the number and position of protons, neutrons, and electrons, all elements with their unique atomic numbers adopt fixed patterns with deformations of the space matrix in various sizes and shapes. These deformations get conserved to maintain the existence of atoms of different elements. Furthermore, atoms of elements combine to form molecules through molecular forces, serving as the building blocks for all types of body tissues in living organisms. They are responsible for building different organs necessary for the smooth functioning of the body, with the sole aim of nourishing the brain; the cage of the soul.

Due to the difference in size, shape, and density (contraction) of the deformed area of the space matrix involved, the elements and the molecules formed exhibit different physical and chemical properties; the same property is defined in conventional knowledge: 'The outermost orbit of valence electrons in an atom is responsible for all the chemical and physical properties of the element.'

Have you ever seen a school of piranhas or a group of thousands of birds flying close to each other in water or the sky? Similarly, our body consists of nucleons spread across various wavelengths in different patterns, shapes, and numbers. The nucleons are accompanied by orbiting, quantum-entangled electrons. All of these components are bound together within mould of EM, atomic, and molecular forces and move as a cohesive unit, 3D printed on the space matrix."

I said, "Now I can understand the procedure by which they constituted your body."

The alien said, "I understand your concern, and you're right that without a basic understanding of the 'working model of our universe, i.e., matrix,' and about the basics of all four fundamental forces, comprehending the operation of reconstructing bodies is impossible. The insight I will further provide you should open your eyes to a whole new understanding of reality, one that was previously unimaginable.

As you pass on this knowledge to the readers of your manuscript you are preparing with our daily discussions, you'll be offering them a glimpse into the workings of the universe, or helping them to see the face of our working god, far beyond our current comprehension, where seemingly impossible feats become reality through advanced technologies and an understanding of underlying cosmic principles."

(3) What is the difference between you and me?

As I asked the question, she further elaborated: "As such, both bodies are designed to support the function of our brains, which are regulated by the power of the soul, just a deformation of the matrix produced by a beam of electrons.

In your body, your heart pumps nutrients and oxygen to your brain to keep it working, and the brain sends impulses to keep the heart, lungs, and other organs functioning properly. As sensory organs, your eyes absorb the visible part of electromagnetic radiation, and your middle ears sense gravity and detect vibrations in the air as sound.

On the other hand, my body works somewhat like plants on Earth. I have stomata all over my two lobes; my upper oblong lobe absorbs oxygen and water, and the lower one absorbs carbon dioxide and water. To utilize this supply from both lobes, we use sunlight as my sole source of energy; EM energy in photon packets acts as 'excitons' to initiate the process of photosynthesis, and thus I can produce all the necessary nutrients. The upper sphere supplies oxygen to my large brain, which is located throughout my upper sphere. The atmosphere and composition of air on Earth exactly match that of my planet.

We both have souls and nervous systems, but we receive all types of electromagnetic radiation and sound vibrations through our coverings of my oblong upper lobe. Instead of blood and blood vessels, we have lymph-filled chambers and channels that supply nutrition to every cell. We shed our skin approximately once every Earth year to remove toxins and waste. However, we reproduce our babies just like you."

(4) What is God?

As I asked her, "Can you tell me about God?" she suddenly and unexpectedly pointed to my laptop (computer) and asked if I could connect her to our cyberspace. She said, "Although I had been connected to your cyberspace during some experiments earlier, first I want to know the standard of your full knowledge."

I was quite surprised by her request, but after deep thought and receiving assurance that after knowing all our pitfalls she would not be hostile to the human race and would not cause any damage to our cyberspace, I agreed.

She said, "Okay, I will extract the entire present knowledge of the human race stored in your cyberspace, and then it will be easier for me to respond to this or any other question you have."

I helped her connect to our cyber world, and I noticed that she was fully engaged with her helmet on. An hour passed, then two, and suddenly she raised her head and said, "Are you ready now?"

I replied, "Yes."

She then explained, "You people talk a lot about God, but have little to no understanding of God."

In short, what we discussed was that she believed we created God out of our fears—fears of suffering, illness, pain, poverty, and darkness. These fears compelled us to search for hope or solace, and we illusioned the existence of a higher power that would help us. She pointed out that we even try to bribe this imagined God with various offerings and seek to please our personal gods through prayers and praises.

She stated that our society lives in myths—myths about gods, religions, relationships, and most importantly, myths about happiness. We assume and take for granted that happiness is not meant for us, and we feel comfortable in our unhappiness, considering it normal. Happiness becomes a taboo in our society.

She then unexpectedly asked me, "Can you tell me how you can create happiness and become happy?"

In response, I immediately remembered and narrated a small incident to the alien. "One cold evening, full of frost, when the lights were fading, one old man was selling cookies in our street. When he passed in front of our house, my wife observed him and asked our servant to stop him. When he approached the gate of our building, she inquired why he was selling cookies while walking in chappals without socks at this time in winter, when it is too cold.

He replied, "I have only one daughter, and after the death of my wife, she asked to transfer the house in her name, and a few months after the transfer of the house in her name, she and her husband kicked me out of the house. So, I am living in a hut outside town. I used to buy 50 cookies in the morning and sell them on the streets at double the price. When I sell all, I go back to my hut, and now it is only six remaining that I have to sell." My wife purchased all six cookies and inquired if he would accept a pair of old socks. He nodded happily, and as my wife returned with one pair of old socks, he put the socks on to cover his cold feet instantly in front of us.

The Cookies was of no use to us, so she distributed it among neighbours' children.

But that night, my greatly satisfied wife said to me "it was best purchase of my life"; she was really happy with her self-esteem boosted by helping one.

Alien said right, you only could become happy when you make someone happy, it is secret of happiness.

(5) Define your God

She asked me "first you define me, your god".

I explained her that there's no concrete description of God in most of literature available, except in the four ancient Vedas, as they predate any religion and thus belongs to all humanity as ancestral knowledge of every human born on Earth. Vedas 'means knowledge' and said to be "spoken by God" (by which God, does it mean some alien) and labelled as **SHRUTI** (which were heard, but from whom) and was remembered by heart from generations to generations before they could be finally written by Ved Vyas in 1500 BC.

The Vedas gave birth to Sanatan Dharma, *the Hindu Science of Living*, but are not tied to any particular religion. Sanatan Dharma, the oldest spiritual practice, is still followed in northern India, in the region once called *Aryavrat*. Its foundation can be divided into **Shruti**, "which has been heard" and its walls are made up of **Smriti**, "what to be remembered."

The Yajurveda 40/8

Describes God 'as omnipresent, omnipotent, with no shape or match, indivisible, creating time and its end, penetrating everywhere, creating and destroying everything, never born nor

---

FOOT NOTE – (description of Sanatan literature)

SHRUTI consists of FOUR VEDAS

(1) RIGVEDA

(2) SAMVEDA

(3) YAGURVEDA

(4) ATHARVAVEDA

dying, knowing your thoughts, reacting to every action, act on principles with purposeful actions, and cannot be confined'.

Each Veda is divided in three or four parts

(!) MANTRA (collection) or SAMHITA (Chanted for Devas)

(!!) BRAHMANAM (Rituals and performance of ceremonies)

(!!!) UPANISHAD (11 Philosophy books on supreme and separated self, on men and universe, on bondage and liberation)

(!V) *TANTRAM (This fourth vanished part is UPAVEDA; is now lost science).*

SMRITI or DHARM SHASTRA (laws to govern persons and society) are also in its four Literatures.

(a) MANUSMRITI (Laws to govern Society)

It divides the period in 7 Manu and tells that we are living in 4 th Manvantaras.

(b) YAGNAVALKYA SMRITI (how to perform Yagna)

(c) *Shankha Likhita smriti (is now lost literature)*

(d) *Parashara smriti (is now lost literature)*

Another two parts of HINDU literature.

(1) **PURANAM** (historical stories)

(2) **ITIHAS** (history)

(A) RAMAYAN (story of RAM) (B) MAHABHARAT (Story of Kauravas and Pandav, the great war and it also includes the GEETA)

Science – in Vedas Science is divided into 6 parts Shad-angani (six-angas or its six limbs) it includes grammar, philosophy, astrology, poetry together with 64 sciences and arts.

(1) Philosophy – is again divided into 6 parts SHAD-DARSHNANI (six darshan or six ways of seeing things or six systems.

They all have one object: putting an end to pain by enabling the separated Human selves to reunite Supreme self, by one method of GYANAM or knowledge.

(2) Nyaya – all things are to be studied by six senses or by inference and analogy or by *testimony* of others.

(3) Shankya – (Purushah or Sprit and Prakritih or matter)

How God made all material world made up of atoms and molecules and how the most useful knowledge of God who is also innermost sprit of man can be obtained in different ways.

(4) Yoga – Yoga is a group of physical, mental and spiritual practices or disciplines to control and still mind.

(5) Mimansha – (what is Karm or duties)

(6) Vedanta – Study of true nature of *God* and *Atma* (Soul), or *Jiva* is essence of same as the innermost god. Man can live on *karma*, which does not bind him, and understanding what *Maya Shakti* is of God, and how to merge with supreme *Moksha* after death.

May be due to her gained access to our cyberspace, the alien then proceeded to briefly comment herself on various religions which all originated only after the compilation of the **Vedas around 5600 BC**, as sagas of many rishis. Thus, Vedas belongs to everyone born on earth, it has no description of incarnation Ram, of Hindu religion.

She said "All the religions, are connected with one or other legendary figure, have their respective books, teaching ideal ways of living, based on the exemplary lives of these incarnations.

In the **oldest religion Hinduism**, the first incarnation was Ram born on 10th January 5114 BC (epic is Ramayana), and Krishna was born on 19th July 3228 BC. Their stories are told in the books Geeta and Mahabharat.

In ancient Egypt (from 3100 BC onwards), the **Egyptian culture worshipped Sun god** and various deities, symbolizing almost everything in sight, including creatures like crocodiles and snakes, which could have instilled *fear* in the layman's mind. *The Pharaohs were considered living gods*, and some even incorporated the name Ram in their titles.

Judaism, which dates back to the Bronze Age (2000 BC), later gave rise to both Christianity and Islam. Judaism, which includes the Tanakh or Old Testament, Talmud, and Midrash. **Zarathustra** dates back to around 1500 BC.

Gautam Buddha, the founder of **Buddhism**, was born on 8th April 623 BC and the religious book is Tripitaka.

Confucius (551-479 B.C.E.) started **Confucianism** in 510 BC, and Lao tzu started Taoism in the 4th century B.C.E.

Jesus Christ was born in 0 BC started **Christianity** and book is Bible, Mohammad started **Islam** in 570 AD book is Quran, and Guru Nanak started **Shikh Dharam** in 1469 AD book is Granth Sahib."

She analysed this knowledge, and remarked that most religions were created long after the Vedas were compiled. Each one arose from stories of significant figures and taught ideal ways of living. She also noted that *myths* and *religious stories* of mythology distorted all religions and even the ancient science of Vedas, leading to complete misunderstanding.

Throughout history, powerful individuals such as kings or priests have used fear as a tool to deceive the masses and create different images of God before the ignorant masses.

Even the Vedas, which means knowledge or Vedic science, were not immune to this influence of mythology. The names used in different descriptions of creation in Vedas were later attributed as Hindu gods in mythology.

(6) **Mythology did not spare VEDAS**

Although the terms used in the description of creation in Vedas have acquired different meanings over time, and mythology converted them in different Hindu gods, but the fundamental characteristics of each god were kept intact.

The *Nasadiya Sukta* (Hymn of Creation) from the Rigveda, the 129th hymn of the 10th Mandala, describes *SAD BRAHMA* (the primordial soup of energy particles) transforming into *ASAD BRAHMA* (forming the omnipresent net of regulatory energy of the universe, also known as the space matrix).

The first division of space matrix produced *Kshir Sagar* (the largest ultra-massive black hole), and its center was named VISHNU (the gravitational center or point 'A' in the Vedas), supported by thousands of *Ishani* (kinetic coloumns). Over time, these kinetic energy channels were described in mythology as a serpent with 1,000 heads, known as *Shesh-nag*. Its operator at the highest energy condensation point became VISHNU, rightly called the god of energy.

The uncurl *Voids*, constantly uncurling to expand universe which symbolizing aging and eventual destruction, are represented by SHIVA, the god of destruction.

Thus, the three gods of Sanatan Dharma—BRAHMA, VISHNU, and SHIVA—came into being.

INDRA was the name of the 'mass unit' (i.e., 35.012 MeV, Unit Electron + 68.5 times space matrix) in the Vedas, that its integral multiples form all visible matter, is rightly regarded as the king of all Dev (DEV is general name given to all elements and also to their unlimited number of compounds).

GANESH, the name of the *unit electron*, is considered the building block of all visible matter.

RUDRA symbolizes rotating black holes that consume stars and matter, churning them out, to flatten the space matrix, by eliminating the wrinkles in the matrix that initially supported this matter by kinetic coloumns.

The SEVEN LOK and SEVEN PATAL LOK are names used to describe the seven *f*-orbits. These are part of the four atomic quantum levels (*s* 1, *p* 3, *d* 5, and *f* 7 orbits), in four set of kinetic coloumns that are formed in the deformation and counter-deformation of one unit space matrix. Each orbit is filled with a pair of positive-spin and negative-spin electrons, forming the 120 elements (DEV) as described in the periodic table.

(7) Where is God?

I asked, "Then where is God?"

She replied, "While atheists may deny the existence of God, it's hard to dismiss the supernatural power governing the universe. To understand this power, we need to explore the laws of nature and how they work.

God, as you define it, is an invisible, omnipresent, omnipotent force. It governs the movement of planets, gives life to all beings, and reacts to every action. This energy, is the generator, operator, and destroyer of the universe."

She then asked me, "If this net of chromodynamic energy of the universe fits your description of God, would you call 'space matrix' as God?"

I replied, "Yes, I would. Why not? Then I have no choice left, but to believe."

She then explained that this "God, is found within the fabric of space itself—an omnipresent space matrix made of minute TREO particles, visualize it as a mosquito net, of positive energy (Treo) woven with negative energy (VOIDS). This matrix is governed by the 'Cosmic Code,' first hinted by Max Planck in 1900 when he introduced the concept of Planck units, as Planck's frequency. Planck's units are the alphabets of HIS cosmic script which waited for a full century to be deciphered by earthling like you."

She continued, "We too use the same units with different names on our planet. However, Mr. Planck, while calculating their values as Planck's units, couldn't identify the meaning behind these units as 'the alphabets of creation' or what they truly represent. The 'Cosmic Code' is determined by the rhythm of the universe's vibrations at Planck's frequency, which controls the workings of the universe. Everything has been meticulously and precisely written in HIS cosmic language, using Planck units bound by the pattern of the Cosmic Code.

Newton, Galileo, and other early scientists believed that by uncovering the underlying patterns of nature—the properties of the space matrix—they were catching a glimpse of God's mind. They saw the elegant mathematical form of these patterns as a manifestation of God's rational plan for the universe. Einstein was on the right path when he said, 'I want to know HIS thoughts; the rest are details.'

Now, let's delve into HIS SCRIPT, the characteristics of the space matrix (Space-Time-Energy) known as 'Asad Brahma' in the Vedas, which could also be said as yet untold description of Higgs field."

I demanded, "Then tell me about this Matrix, and how it fits into our definition of God. Also, describe all the properties of this space matrix (or the workings of our God) just to answer my second eternal question, 'Where am I?'"

In reply, she asked me a question: "Can you tell me, when you hit a ball against a wall, who sends it back to you?"

I replied, "Every action has an equal and opposite reaction."

Alien laughed in my helmet and said, "Are you all parrots, repeating this third law of motion, as described by Newton, over and over without trying to understand this basic nature of the space matrix for the last 337 years? Has no one out of you, even thought to explore the 'HOW' behind it?"

She continued, "Through the three dimensions of *space*, we know *WHAT*. By introducing the fourth dimension of *time* into space (three-dimensions of length, breadth, and depth) transformed it in four-dimensional space-time and thus we could understand *WHERE*. But with the addition of a fifth dimension of *energy*, which was done by you, we could know HOW of universe, as it was necessary to convert space-time into the space matrix [Space-Time-Energy], with its three interdependent components: Space, Time, and Energy. **When Space contracts, Time slows down, and Energy is released to support the loads of all visible matter in the universe and to neutralize the any exerted momentum.**

For example, the momentum exerted by your ball on the wall (which itself is 3D printed on space matrix) is countered by an equal number of kinetons in a kinetic coloumn, like small knot of energy particles formed in mosquito net (small contraction of matrix), and which throws back ball to you.

Newton observed few properties of the space matrix, and now we need to understand, *how they are executed.*

(i) 'Every action has an equal and opposite reaction', and thus, he pointed out to the action-reaction mechanism of the matrix. I will describe it in detail.

(ii) 'If a body is moving, it will keep on moving until a retardation force is applied'; he thus uncovered it's another characteristic: propulsion by the medium, which will be discussed in detail.

(iii) Newton, seemingly talked about gravitation and gave the correct value of the gravitational constant, but he could not explain HOW or WHY this force of gravity is produced.

I will recalculate for you the value of the gravitational constant as given by Newton. It actually tells us only the 'area of the space matrix' and we will re-calculate the number of kinetons in this area, which are required to support one kilogram of mass.

(IV) Einstein added one more dimension of time to the three dimensions of space; to convert universe in SPACE-TIME but even he could not visualize one more elusive dimension: the fifth dimension of energy.

Thus, though he rightly said that gravitation is produced by the deformation of omnipresent space-time and described the curvature of this deformation of space in his general theory, but he was still far away from understanding its HOW and WHY, i.e., or the true mechanism of gravitation.

Without the knowledge of ENERGY, which you introduced, as the fifth dimension of the universe first time in 2005, it was not possible to solve, yet unsolved mystery of gravitation. I will tell you, Energy as fifth dimension changed SPACE-TIME, in to SPACE MATRIX; and made it possible to conceive HOW THE UNIVERSE WORKS and to know about quantum gravitation.

(V) While Peter Higgs earlier proposed the concept of omnipresent Higgs Fields way back in 1964 without describing its structure and working, but without its earlier knowledge, you also independently described it as the space matrix with its 3 interdependent components of space-time-energy in your book 'Inside a Wave', 2005.

(VI) The, role of the 'Fine structure constant' as the *quantity deciding factor* of chromodynamic energy, in the formation of 'mass units' remained far away from Higgs' vision. Though he rightly said that bodies gain mass through the Higgs mechanism and suggested that *'some part of Higgs field (or as you described it as matrix) is dragged away by particles to gain its mass, while the photons move freely in this field'*. I cannot say, that he could visualize and presented the 'mass unit' as God's particle.

She continued, I will tell you the role of the universal constant 'fine structure constant' in the universe and will prove the formation of all visible matter as integral multiples of 'mass unit'.

(V!!) Earthlings could know about the accelerated expansion of the universe and they hypothesized Big Bang *without any knowledge of what preceded it,* which resulted in the Big Bang.

(V!!!) You earthlings are perplexed by the workings of the Quantum world, but it is not mysterious; it is misunderstood. The explanation of 'wave-particle duality' as given below will resolve some enigmas of the quantum world, such as the mechanism behind Quantum tunnelling and the Double slit experiment.

(!X) What is termed as Dark Energy and Dark Matter cannot yet be known.

Whatever you research, you only attempt to uncover one or another property of this Space-matrix, but you all have not been able to formulate its fundamental structure and how it functions.

I am still uncertain if your slumbering society is prepared to comprehend this consolidated knowledge, which will alter the course of your science. I will reveal it all tomorrow."

Chapter 7

DAY 4 – ALIEN PHYSICS OF CREATION AND OF WORKING GOD

TRUE PHYSICS, discussed below, is the basics of all sciences including conventional physics, but still not known to humanity.

WHERE I AM?

(A) Three lectures I found in her dress

The following day, in the morning, I asked Grengi what she had scribbled on the strange looking papers in her pocket. I told her I could not read them as they were written in her language with diagrams, which I could not decipher.

She said, "I am a physics professor at a teaching organisation in my city and I am pursuing my research on physics and astrophysics, which is obviously a study of our omnipresent space matrix. I will tell you all that is in the papers by giving you three lectures in three consecutive days to explain everything that you have been searching for in the past three centuries and what you should all know before you die. Thus, I will let you see the face of our working God."

I made sure that all further discussions with the alien were being recorded on my recorder for preparation of my daily notes and I also took photos of some diagrams sketched by hand by her on these papers, to which I re-scathed on my computer.

She started, "*If you reach a dead end on a street, it is better to turn around.*"

She continued "Have you ever wondered, why your understanding of physics, has remained stagnant for so long, especially since the last century on planet Earth.

It was not only due to the ignorance of the fifth dimension of the universe, ENERGY, but also the mistake of using arbitrary SI units to study the universe instead of the already known Planck's units. This has kept your physics at a standstill with no progress in its basics.

I became quite alert when she said I would have to start from the basics.

From your current knowledge in your cyberspace, I can infer that the human race has only observed the universe superficially up until now, and this race is very resistant to any change that goes against the principle of evolution, through which we all formed and improved.

I think you people are experts in complicating simple things. Creation is done by a creator with one object and one tool in hand; it is done meticulously but with only a few simple principles involved.

You try to observe the universe (blinded by the ground glass in your spectacles) as you try to understand it with the KILOGRAM (an arbitrary chunk of iridium metal kept in Paris – France) as the unit of weight and with the METRE (the 40000 th division of the meridian which passes over France) as the unit of length, when you have already known since 1900 AD about universal units such as the 'PLANCK MASS' (a universal unit of MASS) and the 'Planck least length' (a universal unit of LENGTH), and also 'Planck least time' (a universal unit of TIME).

The alien said that her great-great-grandfather's friend had visited planet Earth 5600 BC and influenced the minds of many rishis during their prolonged meditations to impart knowledge, which was subsequently preserved as the Vedas (said to be Shruti, meaning heard from Gods), the four knowledge books. Perhaps it was your turn now?"

LECTURE 1:

Space-time-energy

Structure of our Working God

This chapter discusses the fundamental structure of the universe, presenting a model of space-time-energy (omnipresent Space Matrix) with the introduction of ENERGY as fifth dimension, through the concept of 'Treos' and 'Voids'. Treos are one-dimensional energy particles, which form the 5 positive dimensions of the universe and are woven into a space matrix alongside voids, the 5 negative dimensions.

Key Points of first lecture:

1. **Treos and Voids**: Treos. each of 'Planck least length', form the five positive dimensions, while voids define the negative dimensions. Together, they create a 10-dimensional omnipresent space matrix (woven like omnipresent mosquito net).

FOOTNOTE:

1. Planck's least length lp = 1.616255 × 10^−35 m

2. Planck's least time tp = 5.391247 × 10^−44 s

3. Planck's Frequency 1/ Planck Least Time.

4. Planck's mass mp = 2.176434 × 10^(-8) kg

5. Planck constant h = 6.62607015 × 10^(-34) J Hz^(-1)

6. TREO or strings = 1.616255 × 10^(-35) m (length)

7. Voids = 5 negative dimensions (no length, no breadth, no depth, absorbs energy and universally, simultaneously, constantly uncurling and thus calibrates total passed time.)

2. **Time**: All bound Treos in matrix are vibrating at a cosmic rhythm (Planck's frequency, or S times per second). After each vibration in 'Planck's least time' the universe readjusts, this constant and ongoing change is perceived as 'flow of time'.

3. **Energy**: Energy is the transformation of potential energy stored in vibrating Treos is converted in kinetic energy, used to support loads through 'kinetons', arranged as small knots of kinetic coloumns.

4. **Expansion of the Universe**: 'Curled up voids' absorb this energy to uncurl, which results in expansion of universe, which is indicator of the passage of time and the aging of universe.

5. **Dark Energy and Dark Matter**: Bound Treos (dark energy) make up 68% of the universe, while 25% is kinetons (dark matter) supports 5% visible matter.

6. **Quantum Energy Levels**: Energy accumulates in steps at under root S quantum levels in each of five dimensions, forming all photons, elementary particles, and all cosmic bodies.

7. **Creation Mechanism**: The *action-reaction mechanism*, as one tool of creation governs universe, by its simple principal, all loads of mass/ momentum on the space matrix are actions and equal number of kinetons reacts to support the loads.

8. **Atomic and Cosmic Structure**: Matter and energy are structured through quantum levels, leading to the formation of elements and cosmic bodies, supported by kinetic columns of varying dimensions.

9. **Vedic Connections**: The chapter draw parallels between modern scientific concepts and ancient Vedic descriptions of atomic structures and of fundamental particles.

The lecture emphasizes that space, time, and energy are interconnected through a space matrix, governed by Treos and voids, with dark energy and dark matter in matrix itself forming the majority of the universe.

Text.

(I) **One object of creation – Treos**

The one-dimensional energy particles as treos constitute five positive dimensions of the universe. They were initially compiled alternately with completely curled-up 'voids' (five negative dimensions) to construct the omnipresent SPACE MATRIX (Space-Time-Energy) of the universe. Please refer to Figure 2.

The voids constitute five negative dimensions of the universe. The Voids are necessary to give identity, shape, and place to vibrate for all TREO while they themselves have no length, breadth, and depth. They absorb energy, which is responsible for the slow and simultaneous, identical uncurling of all voids after each vibration in 'Planck's least time'. With this constant uncurling or expansion of each void the universe/voids calibrate the time passed and is responsible for the aging of the universe and all its constituents and creatures, including all of us.

Treos can be divided into two classes. Those bound and arranged alternately in matrix with voids become 'BOUND TREOS', while "FREE TREOS" accumulate and condense at each next quantum level to form PHOTONS and ALL ELEMENTARY PARTICLE packets, or all visible matter.

The bound treos of all space matrices simultaneously and continuously vibrate S times per second at "cosmic rhythm" The (1.855 × 10^43 at Planck's frequency), each time after a gap of one Planck's Least time. S number of vibrations per second of the whole universe simultaneously produces resonance and qualifies 'S number' as another 'new dimensionless universal constant' or the "KEY OF UNIVERSE".

Our space is not empty, but it is a 10-dimensional omnipresent Space-matrix, to which you have conceived till now as 4-dimensional space-time.

(ii) What is SPACE?

Visualize it as something like an 'omnipresent mosquito net' woven with energy particles as identical very small matchsticks called TREO (or in the language of physics, one-dimensional strings of Planck's least length).

If you are asked to create three dimensions of SPACE only from small matchsticks, you would put them in a line to create 'LENGTH', then arrange them as squares to create the second dimension of 'BREADTH', and finally arrange them as cubes to create the third dimension of 'DEPTH', resulting in a three-dimensional space. The SPACE of our universe is an omnipresent matrix of Treos, and these multiple cubes form its layers, one over the other, spanning everywhere.

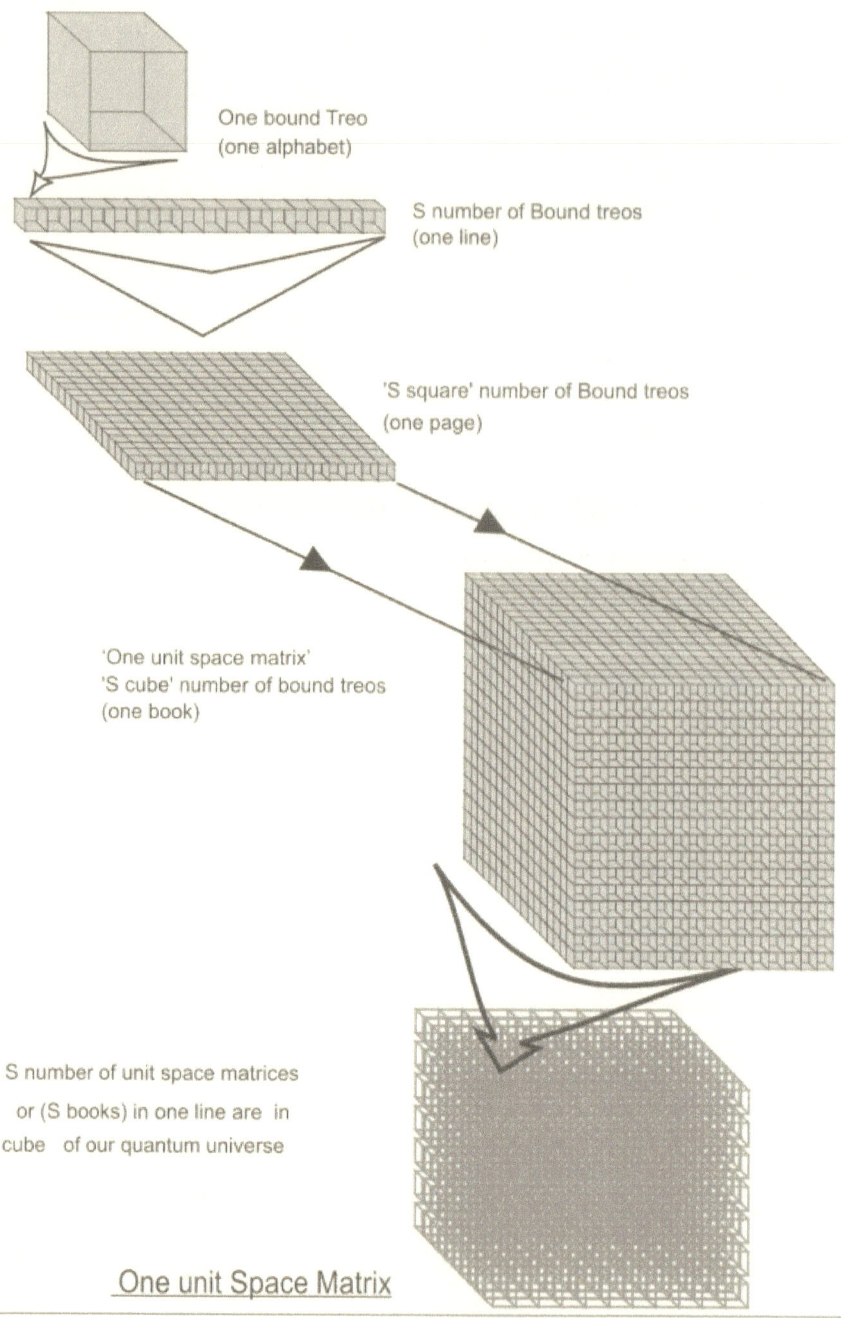

Figure 2 – Visualize the universe as an omnipresent net of bound Treos.

(iii) What is TIME?

In her papers Grengi elaborated on the concept of time as it relates to the structure of the universe and its vibrations.

1. Cosmic Rhythm and Vibrations:

- Time is characterized by the **vibrations of bound Treos** within the omnipresent space matrix, which vibrate **S times per second** at **Planck's frequency**.
- This frequency is described as the **'Cosmic rhythm'**, a fundamental aspect of the universe's structure that dictates the behaviour of all energy particles.

2. Cosmic Code:

- The number of vibrations per second (S) is referred to as the **'Cosmic code'**. Each bound Treo vibrates in multiple directions within a circle, allowing it to participate in all planes of vibration. This spherical representation emphasizes the multidimensional nature of time.

3. Flow of Time:

- After each vibration in the **Planck least time**, the universe undergoes a continuous adjustment, which is perceived as the **'flow of time'**. This constant change is essential for the dynamic nature of reality.

4. Processing Time:

- Every change (whether kinetic, chemical, biological, or physiological) requires this **'least processing time'** or **'least reaction time'**. If a process takes longer than this time, it can lead to a slowdown in the rate of change, indicated by a reduction in the number of vibrations per second in a locally contracted space.

5. Impact of Gravitational Kinetic Energy on Time:

- The alien draws an analogy to GPS technology, explaining that calculations must account for the differences between **'Satellite Time'** and the **slowdown of 'Earth Time'**. This slowdown occurs due to the increased gravitational kinetic energy experienced at the Earth's surface compared to that in a satellite's orbit.
- Failure to account for this difference can lead to significant errors in navigation, as the Earth clock runs slower due to the curvature of space and the resultant reduction in the number of vibrations of local bound Treos.

6. Visualization of Time:

- Figure 3 illustrates how each bound Treo vibrates in multiple directions, creating a complex system of vibrations that spans all S circles within a sphere over the course of S seconds.

The matrix continuously vibrates S times per second (at Planck's frequency) which is the 'Cosmic rhythm' and it also decides S number as the 'Cosmic code', as each bounded energy particle, known as a 'BOUND TREO', vibrates in all possible S number of directions of a circle in one second.

Thus, it will vibrate in all planes of such S number of circles, which can be formed all around in a sphere, to consume its total allotted time (in one lifetime of the universe) of S seconds.

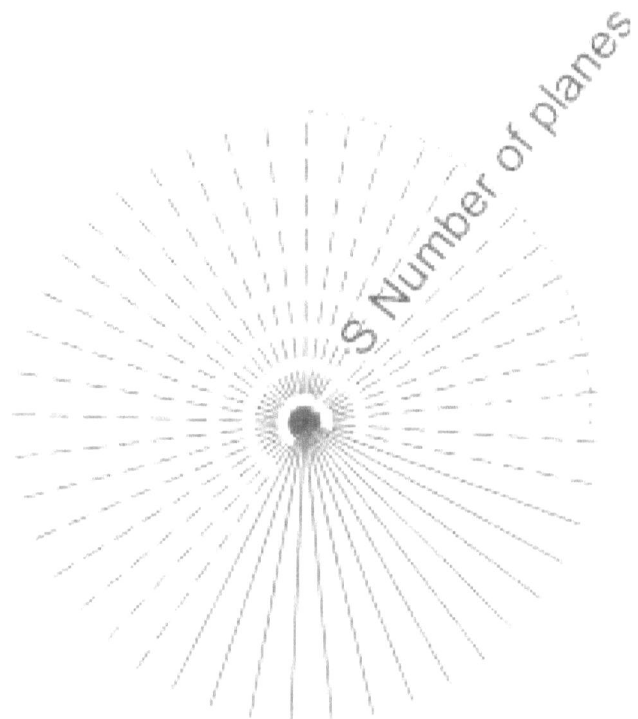

Figure 3 – Each bound Treo is constantly vibrating in S directions of a circle in one second; it will vibrate in S circles of a sphere in S seconds.

After each vibration in the 'Planck least time', the universe re-adjusts itself, continuously changing, which we perceive as the **'flow of time'**.

Every change (kinetic, chemical, biological, physiological) occurs and requires this 'least processing time' or **'least reaction time'**. If any change takes more time, it will slow down the rate of change by reducing the number of vibrations per second in locally contracted space.

Fourth dimension of Time

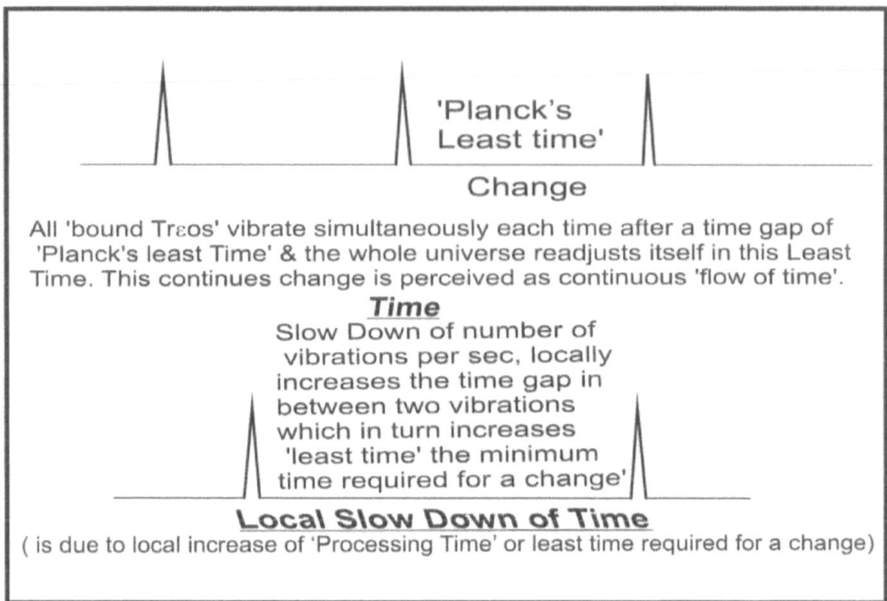

Figure 4 – Slowdown of Time is produced by reduction in NUMBER of vibrations per second in locally contracted area of space.

(IV) But what is ENERGY?

The alien Grengi further elaborates on the nature of energy, its conversion processes, and its interrelationship with space and time, while also exploring the concept of voids and the

---

FOOTNOTE:

In GPS calculations, you take into account the difference of 38 nano second per day between 'Satellite Time' and the slowdown of 'Earth time' caused by increased gravitational kinetic energy on Earth's surface, compared around satellite, in gravitational field of Earth. This is crucial to avoid errors. If time this difference of earth clock and satellite clock is not taken into account the GPS will guide you to the wrong next lane. As Kinetic energy increases by increasing contraction of space towards Earth the *number* of vibrations per second, of local bound treos vibrating in S directions are curtailed, leading to slow down of time and Earth clock will move slow.

composition of the universe. Here's a detailed breakdown of the key ideas presented:

Energy Conversion:

- Energy is defined as the conversion of **LOCAL POTENTIAL ENERGY** of continuously vibrating **BOUND TREOS** into the **KINETIC ENERGY** of **KINETONS**.
- When bound Treos begin vibrating **S times per second**, only in the direction of an exerted load, they transform into **Kinetons**. This process is illustrated in Figure 5, which shows how the vibration of a bound Treo in the direction of a load enables it to support that load.

It is the conversion of LOCAL POTENTIAL ENERGY of continuously vibrating BOUND TREOS into the KINETIC ENERGY of KINETONS. These local bound Treos, previously vibrating in S planes per second, convert into Kinetons, as they start vibrating S times per second only in the direction of the load, to provide it support. See Figure 5.

Figure 5 – When a bound Treo starts vibrating S times per second solely in the direction of the load to counteract the load, it transforms into one Kineton.

(V) Interrelationship of 3 components of SPACE MATRIX: SPACE, TIME, and ENERGY.

Interrelationship of Space, Time, and Energy (Dynamic Interactions):

An increase in load results in **SPACE CONTRACTING**, which involves increasing the number of dimensions one by one. As space contracts, **TIME SLOWS DOWN**, and the **POTENTIAL ENERGY** of the matrix is converted into **KINETIC ENERGY**. The contraction progresses through the dimensions: starting with length, then breadth, and finally depth. Then results in a four-dimensional contraction that includes multiple unit space matrices.

With increasing load, SPACE CONTRACTS (and involves increasing number of dimensions one by one) TIME SLOWS DOWN, and the POTENTIAL ENERGY OF THE MATRIX IS CONVERTED TO KINETIC ENERGY.

First space contracts, to involve length, then breadth, and finally depth, i.e., thus all 3 dimensions of SPACE CONTRACT. Then, the 4th dimension of TIME is also involved, with inclusion of multiple unit space matrices in this contracted area.

(VI) Voids

Nature of Voids:

- The universe originally had no empty spaces or voids. Voids are described as fully contracted **five negative dimensions** devoid of length, breadth, or depth.
- These adjacent voids absorb energy from vibrations to expand themselves and regulate the passage of time. Since the **BIG BANG**, voids have been expanding by **1/S² of their present size**, contributing to the overall expansion of the universe, which is accelerating due to the continuous churning of its matter.

The universe did not have any empty spaces or voids at its birth. Voids refer to empty spaces as fully contracted five negative dimensions with no length, breadth, or depth. The adjacent voids absorb the energy of EACH vibration to expand themselves and also calibrate the passage of time. Since the BIG BANG, the voids have been constantly uncurling in one direction out of the total

S^2 directions possible at each point, increasing by '1/S^2 of its present size'. As a result, our universe is expanding, and with the churning of matter it is accelerating its pace.

(VII) Dark Energy, Dark Matter, and Visible Matter

Composition of the Universe:

The omnipresent space matrix can be visualised as an invisible mosquito net or simply SPACE, woven with **BOUNDED TREOS as DARK ENERGY PARTICLES**, which make up 68% of the universe. All bound Treos vibrate simultaneously at Planck's frequency, determining the baseline potential energy of each 4 dimensions as, **S, S^2, S^3, and S^4** Kinetons respectively.

FREE TREOS constitute 5% of the universe as VISIBLE MATTER.

While 25% of the universe consists of **KINETONS or DARK MATTER PARTICLES** (converted bound treos) to support the LOAD exerted on space matrix in *square* of unit masses of each unit mass of this visible matter.

The rest of the 2% Kinetons constitutes faint Galactic Halo (to hold gas), billions of kilometres long dense cosmic strings, and spinning filaments, supporting and constituting the architecture of the universe.

Any ripples of Space-time, such as gravitational waves or any other waves, are just collections of kinetic columns along their wavelength, all composed of kinetons, visualize them as wrinkles in sheet of space matrix.

(VIII) All Loads of Visible Matter on Space-Matrix

In Our Quantum Universe, √S Quantum Levels are in Each of five Dimensions;

Treos' or **one quantum EM energy** present in a 'Unit Photon'. Integral multiples of one **Mass unit** (under root S quanta Free treos in a unit electron with its 68.5 times matrix) constitute all 5% of VISIBLE MATTER IN THE UNIVERSE.

(IX) √S Quantum Levels Are in Each of Five Dimensions.

EM energy in first dimension and Mass Energy increases in rest of five dimensions, at √**S quantum levels in each of 5 dimensions** (as steps of the staircase).

At all these quantum levels, the accumulation of energy starts from 'one quantum energy' in the first dimension.

And in this accumulation, the maximum value of any one dimension becomes the minimum for the NEXT DIMENSION and works as the 'UNIT OF INCREMENT' of this dimension.

i.   In the first dimension, the EM energy increases by a unit of 1 quantum (in a **unit photon** as the unit of increment). This process produces √S types of various photon packets that constitute the entire EM Spectrum.

ii.   Then, accumulating as √S quanta of energy (in a **unit electron** as the unit of increment), at each of √S quantum levels, it increases up to one 'UNIT MASS' (Planck's Mass; 2.173 x 10-8 Kg) at the last √S quantum level of the second dimension.

However, two electrons with the same charge cannot unite with each other, resulting in the need for the formation of mass units (unit electron + 68.5 times space matrix as binding energy provided by kinetons).

These 'mass units' created all visible matter, as elementary particle packets, nucleons, and thus atoms of all elements are integral multiples of the mass unit.

This Unit mass is the maximum load that can be supported at any "one bound Treo" in the universe, by one graviton through its graviton column at its 'unit gravitational centre'.

iii. In the third dimension, energy accumulates from S quanta (**'Unit Mass'** as the unit of increment) to a body of $\sqrt{S}$ unit masses (roughly one billion metric tonnes).

iv. Similarly, in the fourth dimension, all cosmic bodies are formed from ($\sqrt{S}$ **unit masses** as unit, in **electron black hole** as the unit of increment) accumulation, to a maximum of S unit masses present in a unit black hole at the last $\sqrt{S}$ quantum level.

v. In the fifth dimension, the unit of increment is S unit masses, which is equivalent to a **one-unit black hole**.

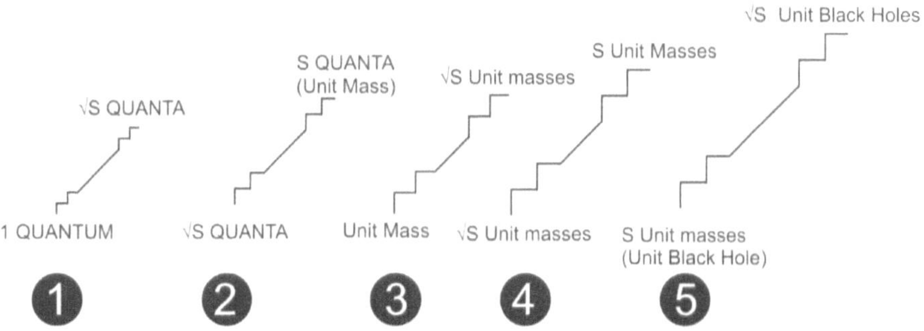

Figure 6 – Show that there are $\sqrt{S}$ quantum levels in each dimension, where energy starts accumulating as one quantum and the maximum value of any dimension reached becomes the unit of increment for the next dimension. This is visualised using the LOG $\sqrt{S}$ scale.

(X) Units of Increment of Energy in all Five Dimensions

- Each dimension has its unit of increment:

In the first dimension, **one quantum energy** is present in one 'unit photon' represented as one unit, which increases at √S quantum levels, resulting in the formation of √S types of photons comprising the entire EM spectrum. Similarly, **√S quanta in 'unit electron', S quanta in 'one-unit mass', and '√S unit masses'** in 'electron black hole' become the units of increment, respectively in the second, third and fourth dimension.

Finally, in the fifth dimension, **S unit masses (one-unit black hole)** serve as the unit of increment to form all galactic centres, super-massive and ultra-massive, to ultimately form Kshir Sagar a collection of √S unit black holes mass [which exert its LOAD in square of unit masses in this body, which is thus supported with total kinetic energy of universe S x (S^4) kinetons, or equivalent to kinetic energy of S unit black holes, acting at its gravitational centre, named as VISHNU in Vedas].

Or VICE-VERSA as described In Vedas that the Asad Brahma first fragmented to form Kshir Sagar, which gets further fragmented, with this concentrated of energy initially formed for a very brief time, when the fragmentation of the matrix started of our functional unit universe just after big bang, to create all creation.

(XI) <u>Support of loads on Space matrix</u>

One Tool of Creation: The Action-Reaction Mechanism

The **ACTION-REACTION MECHANISM** is fundamental tool in the creation process. It is the one tool used in the entire creation process. ACTION is generated by all types of LOADS (mass or momentum) on the matrix.

While the REACTION occurs through the contraction of the matrix, to generate kinetons which gets arranged as different type of kinetic columns of each dimension to neutralize the exerted loads.

With the neutralization of its load by space matrix, it turns any body into a weightless 'POINT MASS' on the space matrix. This mechanism is fundamental and is the only tool used in the entire creation process.

A simple analogy of the ACTION-REACTION mechanism can be seen when we hit a ball against a wall and observe how it is reflected towards us with equal force.

All photons and mass energy packets, up to one 'unit mass' will spread along their wavelength to exert equal LOAD on each 'apex bound Treo' present along its wavelength. This load as *'free Treos square' and 'quanta square'; (square of its quantum level number)*, respectively in the first and second dimensions is supported, by sub kinetic coloumns and shells, one at each apex bound Treo.

Bodies from, 'unit mass' to 'multiple unit masses, ultra-massive black hole', exert their loads in the *square of unit masses* in the body. These loads are supported at their gravitational centre by an *equal square number of gravitons* in its gravitational sphere around its gravitational centre.

This action-reaction mechanism is the only one tool used in creation.

Figure 7 – The 'free treos' as EM energy in photon packet spreads equally on each 'apex bound Treo' in the wavelength and exert load in 'free Treos square of its quantum level number', which is supported by the equal number of kinetons present in each sub kinetic coloumn which all together form an EM wave.

(XII) Principle followed in all dimensions to support all loads: The formation of supporting kinetic columns to support the load in each dimension is as follows:

- **Kinetic coloumns** are formed to support loads in each dimension, where one-layer increases at each quantum level, defined by specific unit increments.
- The types of kinetic columns correspond to different dimensions:

  - **First Dimension: Sub-kinetic column (unit is one Kineton).**
  - **Second Dimension: Shells (unit is Orbitum, or S kinetons).**
  - **Third Dimension: Electron black hole (unit is Graviton, or S^2 kinetons).**
  - **Fourth Dimension: Gravitational sphere (unit is electron black hole, or S^3 kinetons).**
  - **Fifth Dimension: To form the 'Kshir sager' is largest ultra-massive black hole (unit is 'Unit black hole', or S unit masses, or S^4 kinetons).**

(!) To form any kinetic column of the respective dimension, **one layer of kinetic coloumn will increase at each quantum level,** and one wave thus forms at each quantum level in all dimensions.

(!!) They are formed with 'Unit of the respective dimension', arranged according to the proposed column geometry. There are **2n-1 units in any one layer at the nth quantum level and a total of n^2 units in any 'n layered kinetic column'**

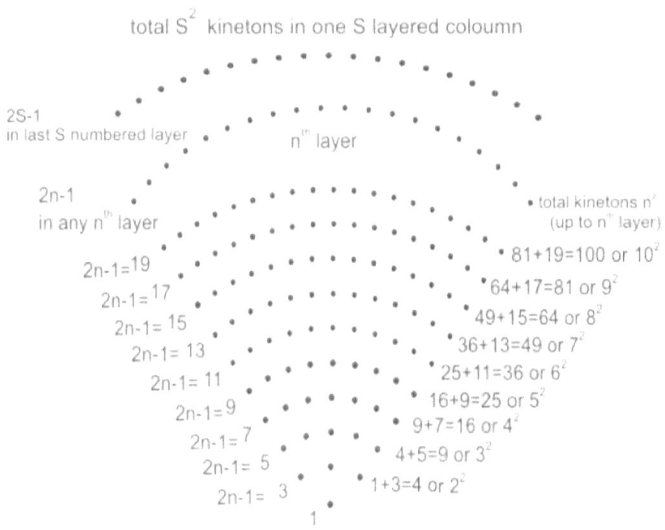

One 'full kinetic /unit gravitational coloumn' follows coloumn geometry
2n-1 in any n^{th} layer and total S^2 kinetons in S layered coloumn

Linear deformation - Coloumn Geometry

Figure 8 – The coloumn geometry which is followed in each dimension: 2n-1 units are in the n th layer and n^2 in the "n layered kinetic column". One-layer increases at each quantum level in each of 5 dimensions.

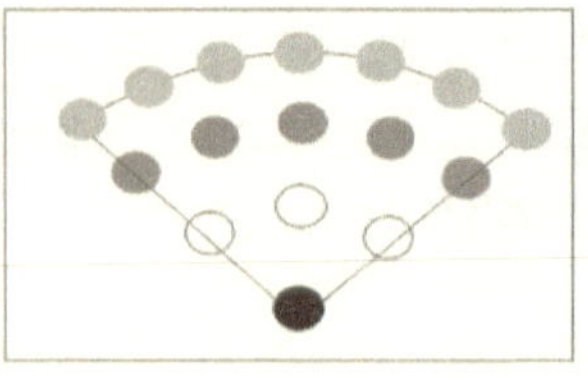

2n -1 Kinetons in first dimension in n th layer
of each sub kinetic coloumn in wave length

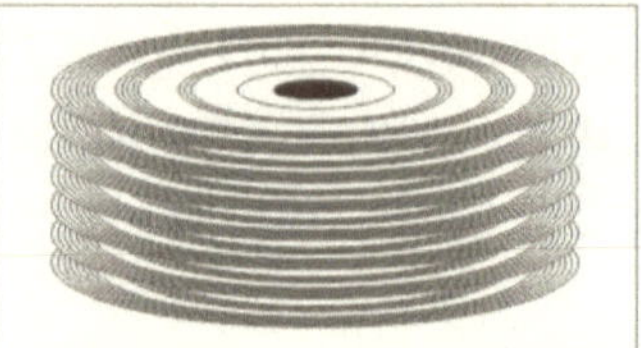

2n-1 Orbitums in second dimension in n th
subshell of each shell in wave length

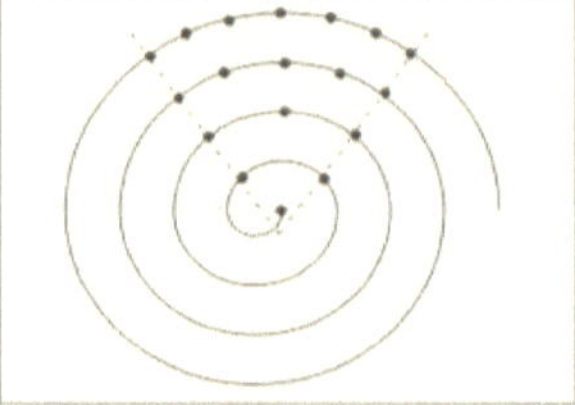

2n -1 Gravitons in third dimension, at n th quantum level (circle) in wave of 'electron black hole'

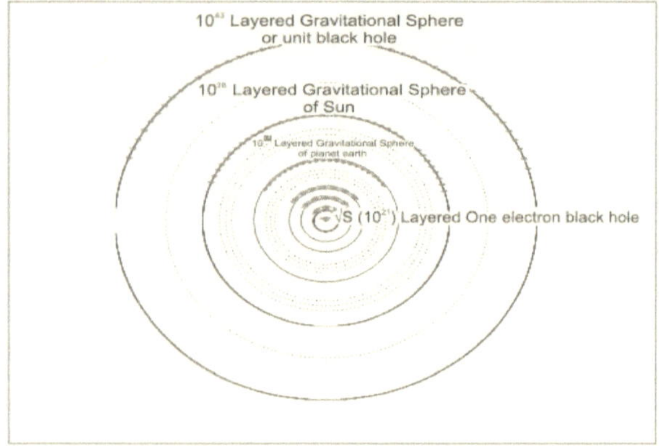

2n- I 'Electron black holes' in fourth dimension at n th quantum
level in 'gravitational sphere' of cosmic bodies

Changing Geometry of deformation in four dimensions of space time

*Figure 9 – Structure of all types of kinetic coloumns; SUB-KINETIC COLOUMN,
GRAVITON COLOUMN, ELECTRON BLACK HOLE and biggest GRAVITATIONAL
SPHERE (or UNIT BLACK HOLE) as kinetic coloumns of all four dimensions
respectively.*

(!!!) Electro-magnetic (EM) energy photon packets produced one-dimensional deformation (in length) and mass-energy packets produces two-dimensional deformation (in length and breadth) to form kinetic coloumns in the quantum world.

The M mass of packets spread along their Reduced Compton wavelength (on 'n apex bound treos') at *Reduced Compton wave length (S number of bound Treo length divided by the number of quanta in the mass-energy packet)*, and exert a uniform load which is supported by kinetic coloumns along full wave which span twice the reduced Compton wavelength (2 n-1apex bound treos).

All thermodynamic transfer is transfer of full layers from donor kinetic coloumn to receiver kinetic coloumn and mismatched portion in length goes as waste energy to Thermodynamic sink (and disperses on matrix).

(!V) In the third dimension, the gravitational load of the body, at its gravitational centre, as square of unit masses which form this body, up to a maximum Load of S unit masses, is supported by "S gravitons" in a solitary spiral kinetic coloumn of the third dimension, which can be described as an "electron black hole." (Refer to photo of Spiral kinetic coloumn in figure 9)

(V) In the deformation of all four dimensions of spacetime, to support a cosmic body of multiple unit masses, which exerts the load (square of unit masses which form body) supported by a square number of gravitons within gravitational spheres around gravitational centre of body. The number of graviton layers in gravitational sphere are always equal to the number of unit masses in any cosmic body.

For instance, Earth's gravitational sphere contains 10^{32} graviton layers, while the Sun's contains 10^{38} graviton layers and unit black hole is supported by a maximum of 10^{43} or S graviton layers; always equals to *number* of unit masses forming these bodies. (Refer to figure 9)

(V!) In case of very larger cosmic structures, such as a galactic centre, supermassive black holes and ultra-massive black holes up to Kshir sagar are supported by increasing number of unit black holes acting as one unit for five-dimensional kinetic coloumn.

With aging and expansion of universe this √S QUANTUM LEVEL of fifth dimension (i.e., total contraction of all dimensions of universe) cannot be re-achieved any more, as it was present momentarily after the birth of universe soon after big bang, with fully contracted space matrix of universe, which soon started dividing; So we will never see Khir sagar (as it, dont exists any more) and its fragments as ultra-massive black holes could be encountered by our telescopes (As looking to our past photo album).

All stars are placed within the *spiral 3-dimensional gravitational field,* of Milky Way's galactic centre, which is supported, by 20 'unit black holes' (a total of 42 million solar masses) in kinetic coloumn of fifth dimension. This spiral structure of galaxy rotates as a disc, causing the outermost stars to rotate at faster speeds (unlike planets which reduces speed with distance as placed in fading two dimensional deformations of gravitational field of Sun).

(XIII) Formation of all elements of the periodic table

1. Formation of Elements:

- All elements are formed through the **filling of preformed empty orbitals**, which can be likened to **electron holes**.
- Each orbital (as it consists of all orbitums of identical energy one over other, along the wave length, half rotating clockwise and other half anticlockwise) can hold one electron of **positive spin** and one electron of **negative spin**.
- This process occurs at the **first four atomic quantum levels**, leading to the formation of four pairs of **kinetic columns** (shells) through the **deformation** and **counter-deformation**

of the **unit space matrix**. This process leads to the formation of all known 120 elements, as described in the periodic table.

○ As shown in Figure 10, four **matter waves** form at the first four quantum levels, with decreasing numbers of shells and wavelengths.

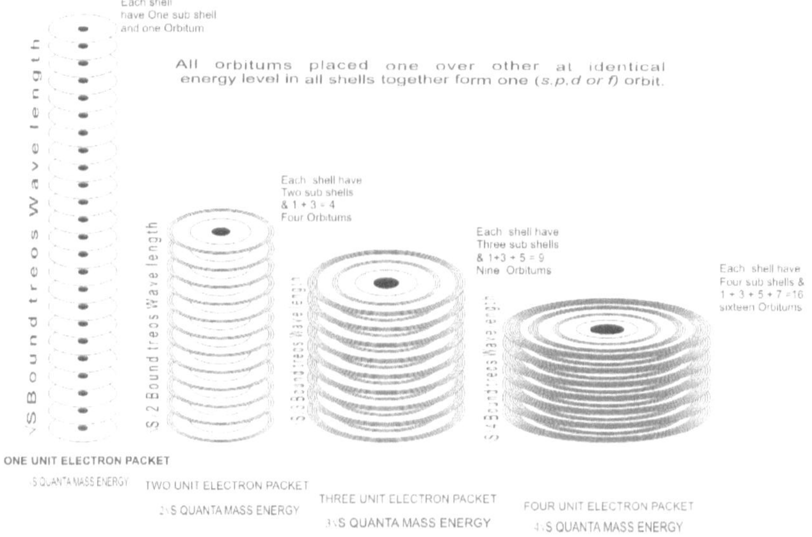

Figure 10 – At first four quantum levels with decreasing wave length; shells have subshells with 1, 3, 5, and 7 orbitums respectively.

○ The subshells consist of:

- **1 orbitum** in the **s** subshell,
- **3 orbitums** in the **p** subshell,
- **5 orbitums** in the **d** subshell,
- **7 orbitums** in the **f** subshell.

○ It leads to the formation of **1, 3, 5, and 7** orbits.

In the formation of all elements, the column geometry in the second dimension of orbits prevails. It forms only four pairs of shells at first four quantum levels in the deformation and counter-deformation of the space matrix (Figure 11).

Thus, 2+2, 8+8, 18+18, and 32+32 quantum entangled electrons, along with an equal number of protons as pair, are filled to form atom of all elements.

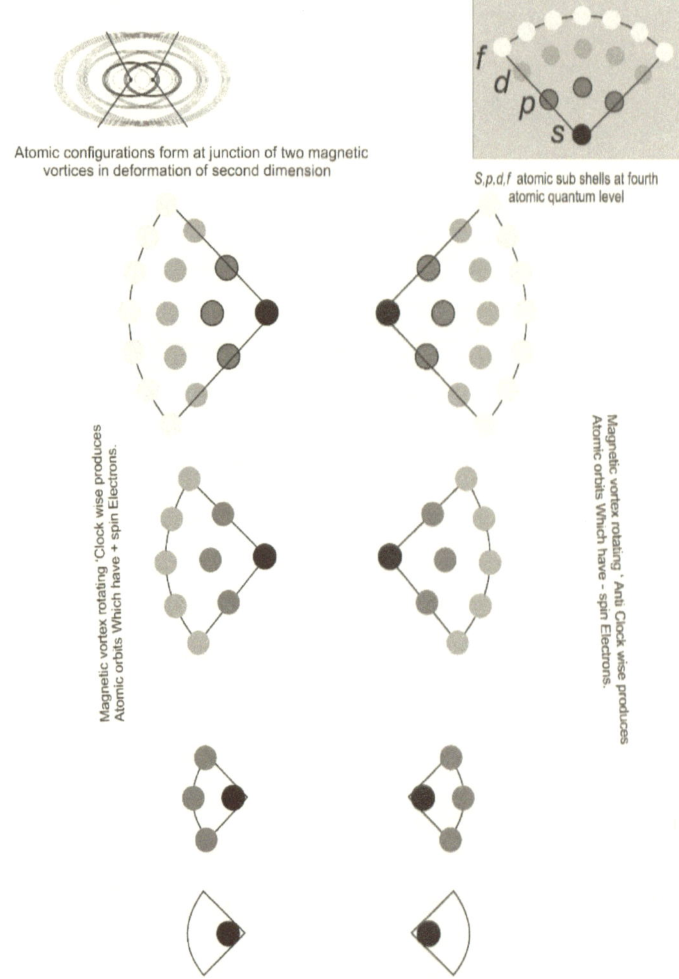

Two magnetic Vortexes rotating in 'clock wise' and 'anti clock wise' rotations form Atomic orbits with + Spin and - spin Electrons which totals 2,8,18,32 at four 'atomic quantum levels'.

Figure 11 – Orbits in 4 pairs of shells which form at four quantum levels in the deformation and counter deformation of the unit space matrix.

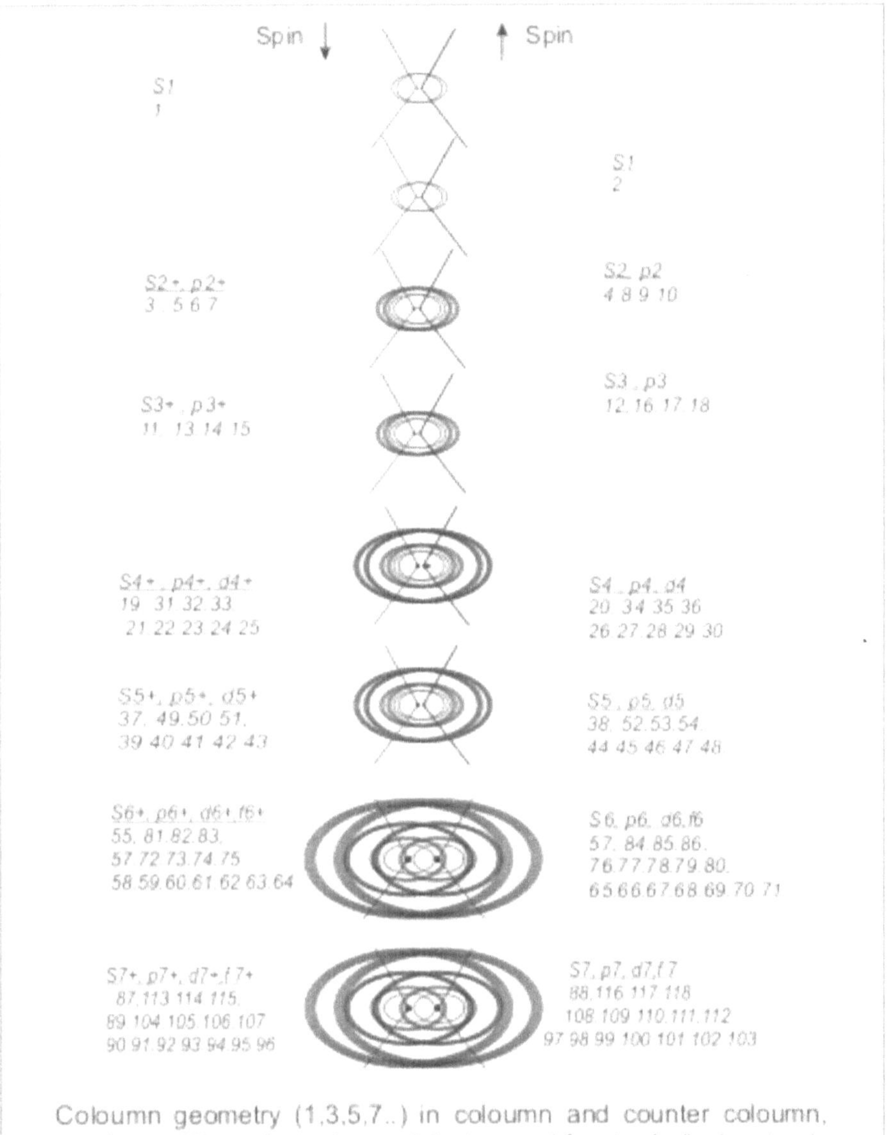

Figure 12 – At the first four atomic quantum levels, the increasing number of s (1), p (3), d (5), and f (7) orbits in sub-shells are filled with both + and - spin electrons in all four pairs of mutually entangled shells. These shells are formed in the deformation and counter-deformation of the 'unit space matrix' to form all 120 elements.

Magnetism:

In matter wave, half of the orbitums rotate **clockwise**, while the other half rotates **anti-clockwise**. This rotational motion creates a magnetic effect, causing the moving electrons to behave as small magnets, referred to as **magnetrons**, with **north and south poles**.

(XIV) Description of modern atomic structure as described in Vedic science*

The 'Palitha' represents the **p** subshell with 3 orbits, 'Asnah' represents the **d** subshell with 5 orbits, and 'Ghrat-Prasthah' represents the **f** subshell with 7 orbits.

In this description of the atomic structure, the seven 'atomic quantum energy *in f subshell* were referred to as Seven Loks, while the adjacent 'counter deformations of atomic energy quantum levels' are Seven Patal Loks.

They also knew about three Mesons as TRI-VATRAMA.

But how did the ancient Hindu scholars (known as RISHI or priests and MUNI or scholars) could know about the six quarks, in 5600 BC as SAT-VRNDARAKAHA (SIX-Quarks) as described in Vedas*; without told by Alien civilization? Hindus could preserve this divine knowledge by remembering all Vedas by heart from generations to generations till they could be written in 1500 BC.

Names of 6 quarks in Vedas (1) TRIDASHAH is Charm, (2) AGNISVWATA is Strange, (3) YAMYA is Up, (4) TUSHITA is Down, (5) PARINIRMIT VASVARTIN is Top, (6) and APARINIRMIT VASVARTIN is the name of the Bottom quark.

Chapter 8

DAY 5 – COSMIC CODE

LECTURE 2:

'I want to know HIS thoughts, rest are details', Einstein.

Key Points of second lecture:

S number; new dimensionless universal constant

The chapter introduces the "Cosmic Code," a concept representing the hidden symmetry in the universe, regulated by a new dimensionless constant called "S number" (Saxena's S number).

This constant decides 'unit space', 'unit time' and 'unit mass' (PLANCK'S MASS) and also value of all universal constants, as calculated in appendix for Planck's constant, the speed of light, and gravitational constant.

(A) Number S:

- The S number defines the vibration rate of bound Treos (particles) in matrix of the universe at PLANCK'S FREQUENCY, leading to its significance in unveiling the basic functioning of universe, along with determining the values of all universal constants.

(B) Propulsion by Medium:

- **All supports and propulsion in the universe occur over 'one unit of time' (S vibrations, equivalent to one second).**

(C) Waves (EM, Matter, Gravitational):

- All waves (electromagnetic, matter, and gravitational) serve to support all loads.
- Load of any number of Treos is supported by equal number of Kinetons in kinetic coloumns present at each apex bound treos along its wave length, and thus formed the structure of the waves, with locally balanced angular momentum.

(D) Wave-Particle Duality:

- The chapter elaborates on how particles can behave both as waves (spread) and particles (condensed), which explains many unexplained phenomena of quantum word, like quantum tunneling and the double-slit experiment.

(E) Mass Units:

- 'Mass unit' is unit electrons + with 68.5 times binding energy, and all elementary particles and nucleons like protons, are its integral multiples.

Finally, the chapter delves to explain why protons and other nucleons derive most of their mass from binding energy rather than quark energy, which contributes only one percent.

Text.

In order to understand the regulatory note that governs the pattern of the universe, we must first understand the "Cosmic Code," which regulates the hidden symmetry of creation.

(A) Number 'S'

According to Planck's frequency, all bound Treos in the universe vibrate simultaneously at a rate of 1.855×10^{43} or 'S times per second' at Cosmic rhythm. This gives us a new dimensionless constant known as the S number or the "Cosmic Code."

The S number, which is a new dimension less constant introduced, is the key to the universe it regulates universe and assigns values to all universal constants, as calculated. The **unit space** is defined as the cube of the S number of Treo on its one side, which is the area which initially but systematically contracts in response to any load exerted. The **unit time** is defined as the S vibrations of Treo, which is equivalent to one second. The **unit mass** is defined as S^2 Treos, which corresponds exactly to Planck's mass (2.176×10^{-8} Kg).

Value of all universal constants is decided by "Cosmic Code."

(i) The reduced Planck constant and Planck constant:

The S number of free Treos represents one quantum of electromagnetic energy, while the S number of bound Treos generates one quantum of potential energy. The S number of Kinetons, which are deformed bound Treos, constitutes one quantum of kinetic energy.

S number of Treos calculate the reduced Planck constant, while its angular momentum corresponds to the value of the Planck constant. (refer appendix A calculation 1)

(ii) The speed of light:

The speed of light is determined by the transitional motion of photons. With each vibration, the photon packet is pushed to the next bound Treo, and this determines the speed of light, which is the **distance covered by S bound Treos in S vibrations or per second.** (refer appendix A calculation 2)

(iii) The new derived value of the gravitational constant is derived from the conventional value of gravitational constant (as calculated by Newton) it dictates; **S^2 free Treos in a unit mass is supported by S^2 number of Kinetons in one graviton coloumn per second per second.** (refer appendix A calculation 3)

(B) Propulsion by medium

Propulsion is done along with the **support of all loads which takes one unit time of S vibrations, which is equivalent to one second.**

A packet of one quantum EM energy in a "unit photon" spreads across S apex bound Treos along its wavelength and is supported by S vibrations, of one layered, S number of kinetic columns, which together form an EM wave, of **frequency 1** per second, while simultaneously moving it by S bound Treos distance in one second with the wave, as deformation keep on forming and progress by exerted load of moving photon packet.

An increase in the number of quanta of EM/mass energy in the packet results in an increased number of rotations and units of angular momentum, which is calibrated by Planck's constant, and results with the formation of *equal number of EM waves* or by *equal total number of rotating orbitums* in a matter wave.

Each quantum of EM/ mass energy in a packet is supported from S directions in a circle, either by one rotation of one EM wave in the first dimension or by one rotation of one orbitum (S kinetons) in the matter wave, in the second dimension in S vibrations of one second.

Being supported by EM waves (with a wavelength greater than the frequency), EM energy packets of photons are simultaneously **propelled at the speed of light**, in translational motion in the first dimension.

With an increasing number of quanta in the packet, equal number of EM waves are formed, which also equals to the frequency of the wave and the number of rotations of packet per second.

As the load increases up to a gamma photon (√S quanta EM energy; √S bound treos wave length equals √S frequency and will form √S EM waves in one second to get it supported in one second), each quantum in any 'photon packet' needs one EM wave to be supported while all quanta in packet are supported by equal number of EM waves in one second.

After the frequency and wavelength equal in the gamma photon, the frequency starts to increase more than the wavelength in the second dimension for all mass energy packets and EM wave converts in matter wave; with kinetic coloumn rotating at its place and thus converted to orbitum. Each quanta mass is supported by one orbitum through its one rotation in one second.

(C) Waves (EM, Matter Wave, and gravitational wave)

*"**All waves are formed to support and push all loads by the Space matrix, judiciously**."*

(!) <u>**EM wave**</u> – All kinetic coloumns supporting load on all apex bound treos spread along wave length of all packets from unit photon (1 quanta) to unit mass (s Quanta) forms EM and MATTER Wave,

(!!) WAVELENGTH of wave = (length of spread of ANY EM Or MASS ENERGY PACKET) = S bound Treos / number of quanta in packet.

(!!!) FREQUENCY = Number of quanta in packet. = It also equals the number of 'layers in sub kinetic column' in each EM wave = the number of EM waves forms per second, or the total number of supporting 'orbitum' in the matter wave, = and the orbital speed or the 'number of bound Treo distance per second'.

(!V) **Matter wave**

Angular momentum for unit electron increases to 45 degree and thus its packet spread vertically and is supported by matter wave by one shell at each 'apex bound Treo' in its vertical wavelength placed one over other.

But in order to be supported in the second dimension, vertically placed any mass energy packet requires one vibration in each shell which are present at each apex bound Treo along its wavelength in its matter wave (now wavelength is less than its frequency) **as supportive force**; *while particle remains still in its orbit.*

Only then is this packet pushed by the next vibration to the next bound Treo in its orbit as **propelling force.** This process is repeated many times, in all S vibrations per second, and thus the point mass moves in its orbit by number of bound treos in one second which is equal to this frequency, and thus, Earth in its orbit moves at the 30 Km (1.8443 x 10^39 bound Treos distance) per second (1.8555 x 10^43). **Visualise it a lady moving on travellator at airport gets down 10^39 times (to its sides), for a dance of 10^4 steps, after each one step on travellator traversed.**

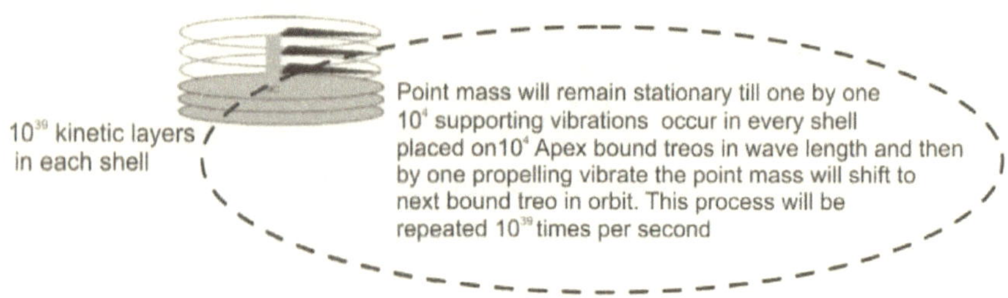

10^39 least lengths (30 Km) in 10^43 vibrations = Orbitarthal Speed of Earth in 1Second

Figure 13 – Point mass of Earth will remain stationary in its orbit, until each (1.006 x 10^ 64) shell in wave length is vibrated by cosmic vibrations one by one with each vibration of universe and then only the point mass in next vibration will shift to next bound Treo.

(V) GRAVITATIONAL WAVE

1. **Gravitational centre** – **Anybody of M unit masses** exerts a load of **M^2unit masses,** which is supported at gravitational

centre by M^2 graviton in a gravitational coloumn which forms around it.

2. <u>**Gravitational field**</u> – While its **2 M load** of this body exerted on each layer of gravitational field spreads and supported by 2M kinetons, present in all 2n-1 kinetic coloumns at each apex bound Treo in this layer which combined together forms the gravitational wave.

(D) Balance of angular momentum in all waves

Each wave locally balances its angular momentum with a counter angular momentum

(!) as Trough and crest forms in EM wave

(!!) as Clock wise and anticlockwise rotations by half orbitums out of the total along wave length, which all together one over other form one orbit in all matter waves; thus, each orbit can lodge one +spin electron, and one-Spin electron in each orbit.

(E) Wave Particle Duality

Simile is 'While in the office you sit compact together (you behaves as particle), but to move back to city you sit in your individual car (you behaves as wave)'.

All 'photon packets' or 'mass energy packets' up to 'one-unit mass' are not point masses, but their EM energy or 'mass energy' spreads evenly across all 'apex bound Treos' on their respective wave along their wavelength.

Furthermore, on top of it, there are two options for the free Treo in the packet: either they can remain **bound together to increase the particle density** in the packet, or each free Treo can **spread on an equal number of kinetons** (one on one) on all supporting kinetic columns, thus becoming part of its wave. (refer to figure 14)

This solves many mysteries of the quantum world, such as the behaviour of photons and electrons in the double-slit experiment of photon and electrons where they *spread* to exhibit as a wave; or photon packet as *condense mass* behaves as particle to exhibit 'Photo electric Phenomenon". For exhibiting the phenomenon of quantum tunnelling the alpha particles behaves as wave and can pass through a nuclear barrier (simile, as big octopus can come out through a slit below the closed door from a closed room).

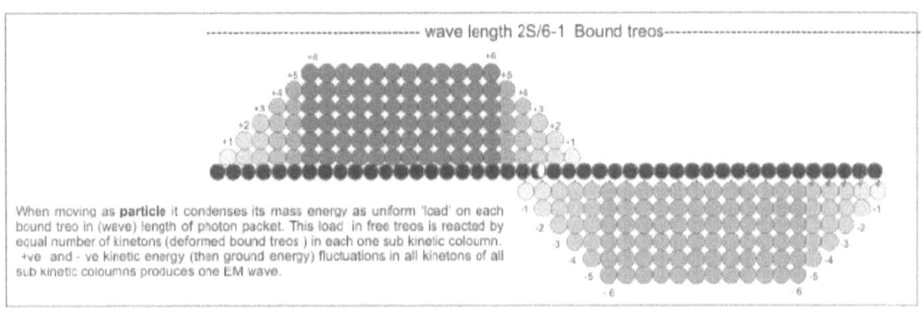

All rotating Sub Kinetic Coloumns (placed side by side) forms one EM wave

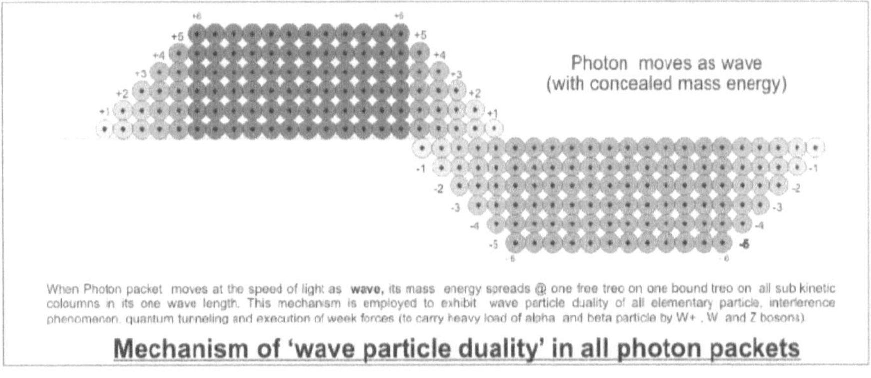

Mechanism of 'wave particle duality' in all photon packets

Figure 14 – Diagrammatic representation to show how Photon exhibits wave-particle duality in an electromagnetic wave:

As a particle, its electromagnetic energy spreads equally on each apex bound Treo along its wavelength and remains condensed.

As a wave, each free Treo's electromagnetic energy spreads on an equal number of Kinetons (one on one) in all sub-kinetic columns, forming an electromagnetic wave.

(F) <u>One mass unit, 35.012 MeV</u>

However, a question arises regarding HOW two negatively charged unit electrons can be packed together (both having negative charge due to their anticlockwise rotations)?

The answer lies in the fact that all matter is composed of composite electrons, where each unit electron is associated with 68.5 times its mass as its binding material. This binding material, known as chromodynamic energy, comes from the space matrix in the form of deformed bound treos.

Figure 15 illustrates this concept using the analogy of bricks and their binding cement material. In this analogy, each unit electron is like a brick, and 68.5 times matrix as cementing or binding material, come together to form one mass unit. **This amount required is calculated by multiplying the mass energy of electron with twice of value of fine structure constant.**

Therefore, each of us possesses 68.5 times the chromodynamic energy, which acts as our driving force, and we each have a major portion as Space Matrix only (or of our working God).

Analogously, just as a single drop is part of a bucket full of water, we are not only part of the Matrix – we are the Matrix, or part of the

---

FOOTNOTE:

(A) According to the table given below the figure 15, all elementary particles and nucleons and thus, all visible matter is comprised of integral multiples of mass units (unit electron masses), table show a deviation of 1% only.

(B) For instance, nucleons (specifically, one proton) are formed by 27 mass units, which can be calculated as 27 × 35.012 ≈ 938.27 Mev, representing the mass-energy of a proton.

This also answers the question of why a proton has most of its mass as 99% Q.C.D or Quantum chromodynamic binding energy, while the contribution of three quarks is only 1% of the proton's mass, 2 × (2.2 MeV) + (4.7 MeV) = 9.1 MeV.

omnipresent God. The Vedas describe this as AHAM BRAHMAS. *"Yatha brahamandey tatha pindaye"*, a drop of water is part of whole water in bucket; or in other words AHAM BRAHAMASHM, it means being part of it, I represent whole universe.

35.012 MeV can be calculated= mass of unit electron 0.511MeV multiplied with the value of twice of fine structure constant (2 x1/137). Thus, Fine structure constants decide the amount of cementing material as binding energy of each electron; which as 'multiple of mass units' form all visible matter.

Figure 15 – We can understand this concept through the analogy of bricks and their binding cement material – the electron as one brick and gluons as 68.5 times its binding material, together forming 'one MASS UNIT'

PARTICLE	Known mass of elementary particles in Mev	Calculated Mass of all elementary particles in Mev	Known mass-calculated mass × 100/ known mass = Error in %	Number of composite unit electron masses in particle as observed here
LEPTONS				
Electron	0.51 Mev	0.51/ 2 (1/137.035999710) = 35.012698 Mev (Composite mass of unit electron or m_e)	0%	= 1
Muon	105.66 Mev	$m_e \times 3$ = 105.3809 Mev	0.26%	= 3
Tau	1776.99 Mev	$m_e \times 51$ = 1785.6475 Mev	0.48%	= 51
MESONS				
Pion	139.57 Mev	$m_e \times 4$ = 140.0507 Mev	0.34%	=4
Kaon	493.68 Mev	$m_e \times 14$ = 490.1777Mev	0.70%	=14
Eta	547.75 Mev	$m_e \times 16$ = 560.2031 Mev	− 0.22%	=16
Rho	775.8 Mev	$m_e \times 22$ = 770.2792 Mev	0.71%	=22
Omega	782.59 Mev	$m_e \times 22$ = 770.2792 Mev	1.57%	=22
Meson	1869.4 Mev	$m_e \times 53$ = 1855.6728 Mev	0.73%	= 53
Ds Meson	1968.3 Mev	$m_e \times 56$ = 1960.7109 Mev	0.37%	=56
B Meson	5279.4 Mev	$m_e \times 150$ = 5251.9023 Mev	0.52%	=150
Bs Meson	5369.6 Mev	$m_e \times 156$ = 5391.935 Mev	0.41%	=156
BARYONs				
Nucleons	938.27 Mev	$m_e \times 27$ = 0945.3427 Mev	− 0.75%	N=27
Lamda	1115.68 Mev	$m_e \times 32$ = 1120.4062 Mev	0.42%	N=32
Sigma	1197.45 Mev	$m_e \times 34$ = 1190.4316 Mev	0.59%	N=34
Xi	1314.18 Mev	$m_e \times 38$ = 1330.4825 Mev	− 0.12%	N=38
Omega	1672.45 Mev	$m_e \times 65$ = 1680.6095 Mev	− 0.48%	N=48
Lamda₂	2284.9 Mev	$m_e \times 48$ = 2275.8254 Mev	0.397%	N=65
Sigma₂	2452.2 Mev	$m_e \times 70$ = 2450.8889 Mev	0.04%	N= 70
Xi₂	2466.3 Mev	$m_e \times 70$ = 2450.8889 Mev	0.62%	N=70
Omega₂	2697.5 Mev	$m_e \times 77$ = 2695.9778 Mev	0.05%	N=77
Lamda*₂	5654.0 Mev	$m_e \times 161$ = 5637.0445 Mev	0.29%	N=161

FOOTNOTE:

All elementary particles and nucleons are integral multiple of MASS UNITS . The table shows it with only 1% deviation.

Chapter 9

DAY 6 – QUANTUM GRAVITY

LECTURE 3:

Key Points of Third lecture:

(1) Quantum Gravity

Why, we could not solve the mystery of gravitational forcesue to following two reasons.

(!) Ignorance about Energy as fifth dimension of universe

(!!) How can a body move uphill, towards higher kinetic energy field.

Quantum Gravity is to support all load of all bodies on space matrix, ranging from unit photons to ultra massive black holes, by load dependent contraction of Space matrix, which involves one by one all five dimensions of universe.

- In contraction of one dimension (in length) supports all photon packets and weak force bosons (W, Z particles) through electromagnetic (EM) and weak force fields. Each photon or boson spreads along its wave length and is supported by contraction as sub-kinetic column at each apex bound treos along its wave length.

- In two dimensions contraction (length and breadth) of unit space, it produces Shells, sub shells and orbitums, to supports matter from 'unit electron' to 'unit mass' by 'matter wave'. Atomic fields are formed with K, L, M, N energy levels by energy in orbitals in s, p, d, f sub shells, of shells which form at four atomic quantum levels.

- For masses greater than a 'unit mass', gravitational forces emerge in the contraction of third dimension (of full unit space) and then in all fourth dimensions (of space-Time) to support earthly and cosmic bodies, respectively.

(2) Gravitational Force

- At the Gravitational Centre: any 'M unit mass body' exerts a load of square of its unit masses (M^2), which is counteracted by equal number of gravitons, present in M number of graviton layers, in its gravitational sphere.
- In a Gravitational Field: The body exerts '2 M unit masses' load on any n th layer of the gravitational field, which spreads on its wave, to be supported by 2n-1 kinetic columns, present at each apex bound Treo along its wave length.
- How can a body Move *Uphill*; or how can a baby body move from lower kinetic energy field to higher kinetic energy field to wards body? This is because the total gravitational kinetic energy in any outer layers is always higher than in inner layers, due to <u>disproportionately increasing value of Factor -1 in inner layers</u> in total number of 2n-1 kinetic coloumns in n th layer; resolves the question of how bodies can move uphill in a gravitational field.

(3) Gravitational Attraction, is fall of bodies towards each other, and results from insufficient kinetic energy and insufficient support (but it cannot be labelled as conventionally said as 'negative gravitational energy') which could be provided to both bodies, by the <u>common shared space matrix in between.</u>

(4) Weightless Point Masses, After being supported by its own gravitational field, all bodies behave as weightless point masses

in the legend gravitational field of parent body, and moves as point mass in its orbit formed by its Compton wave length.

(5) <u>Unification of General Theory with the Quantum World</u> could be achieved.

(6) There is <u>only one force in universe, which manifests as four different basic forces,</u> with local changing geometry which converts the nature and magnitude of force, with the involvement of increasing number of dimensions, in locally deformed space matrix which forms its force field.

Text.

(a) Quantum Gravity

Quantum Gravity is described to support a body (from a unit photon to an ultra-massive black hole) by causing the increasing contraction of the space matrix towards the body in increasing number of dimensions, to counteract its exerted load on the space matrix.

(1) By contraction in one dimension of length, to support photons of the entire electromagnetic spectrum, it forms 'EM fields' and 'weak force fields' for weak force bosons (W Z particles with different charges) inside the nucleus of an atom.

Each photon packet or bosons of weak forces spreads across 2n-1 apex-bound Treos in its wavelength of an electromagnetic wave at the n th quantum level (with n number quanta EM energy in packet) and is supported by kinetons in 2n-1 sub-kinetic columns.

In both fields, one free Treo is supported by one kineton present in respective multilayered 'Sub-kinetic columns' at each apex-bound Treo, after the spread of each packet along its wavelength. These kinetons in all sub kinetic coloumn form the field of Electro-weak forces.

(2) With the contraction In two dimensions, each mass energy packet up to unit mass spreads across 2n-1 apex-bound Treos in its wavelength of a "matter wave" and is supported by 2n-1 shells (kinetic columns of the second dimension) vertically placed one over the other after total increased angular momentum by more than 45 degrees.

To support and form all atoms of all elements, it forms at first 4 quantum energy levels as **K, L, M, N atomic energy levels,** respectively, by *s* (1 orbital), *p* (1+3 orbitals), *d* (1+3+5 orbitals), *f* (1+3+5+7 orbitals) in 1, 2, 3, 4 subshells in shells, to form all 'atomic field'.

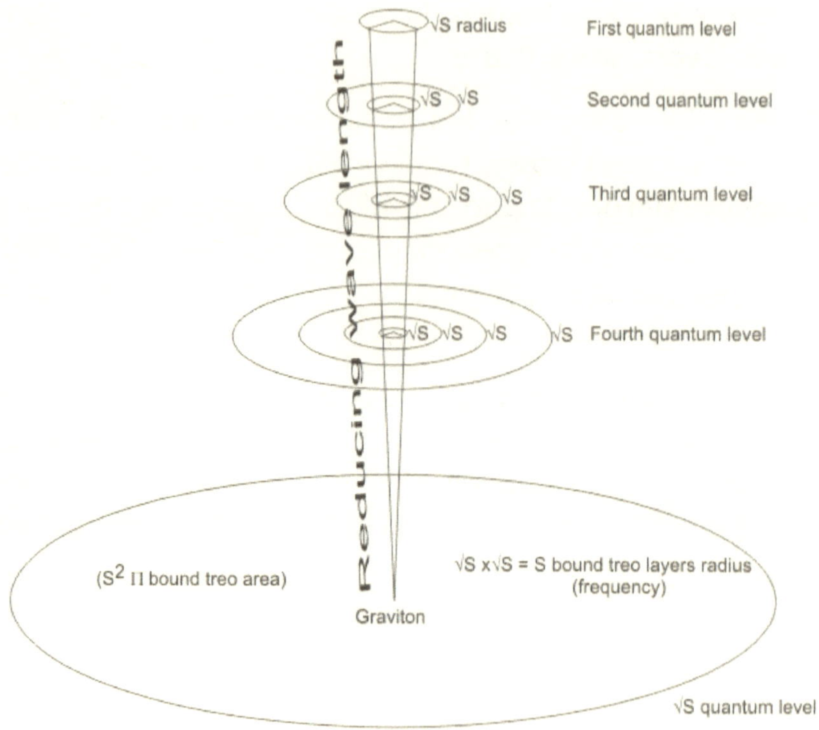

Increasing radius of deformation by √S bound treo layers at each next quantum level

Diagrammatic representation not to scale

Figure 16 – √S number of kineton layers increases to form one sub shell in all shells at first 4 quantum levels.

Similarly, to support increasing loads of more than one unit mass, gravitational forces emerge in the third dimension (3 Knots one over other) to support all earthly bodies, and in fourth-dimensional deformations for cosmic bodies. (i.e., the gravitational sphere which is a kinetic column with a four-dimensional deformation of the multiple unit matrices with deformation of space-time (by 4 knots one over the other).

(3) Gravitational Force

(For details, please refer to page 125 in chapter11 in section position of planets at planetary quantum levels)

(!) At the gravitational centre

A body of M unit masses exerts a Lode of **M^2-unit masses** at its gravitational centre, which is counteracted by **M^2 gravitons** in an M layered 'Gravitational sphere' (a kinetic column in the fourth dimension or a formation of 4 knots).

(!!) In a gravitational field

This body with M unit masses will exerts a load of 2M unit masses on each consecutive concentric layer in the gravitational field, which similarly spreads across 2n-1 apex-bound treos in the n th layer from the gravitational centre (at 'n' radius).

This load is supported by 2n-1 kinetic coloumns present one each at all "apex-bound Treo" in the wavelength of the gravitational wave of this layer. The angular momentum of the wave gives the Compton wavelength or circumference of this orbit. Thus (1), (2), (3) explains the concept of quantum gravity.

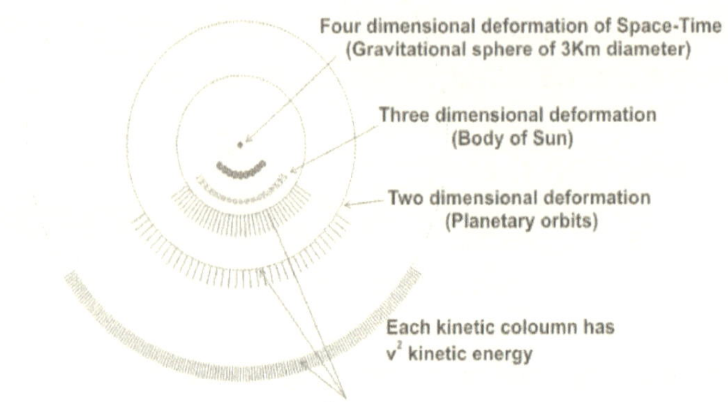

Figure 17 – In each consecutive concentric layer in the gravitational field at any n bound treos distance (radius) on its 2n-1 kinetic columns supports a total exerted load of an 2M unit mass of M unit masses body, the same 2M load is exerted on each layer in the gravitational field till it ends (Total layers in gravitational field of Sun under root S quantum levels x 10^38unit masses in body of sun).

(b) How can a body move uphill?

This is the **first myth and the first unsolved mystery of gravity**, that how and why does a baby's body move from a lower kinetic energy field outside to a higher kinetic energy field towards the body (in simpler terms, will move uphill)? This raises the question that humans have been unable to answer, and thus, gravitational force has always remained mysterious, and the concept of quantum gravity has been elusive.

The million-dollar answer to this question is that the total **gravitational kinetic energy is always higher in any outside layer than the total gravitational kinetic energy in the next inner layer in any gravitational field.** This is due to the disproportionately increasing value of the factor -1 while calculating the total kinetic energy on 2n-1 kinetic columns present in each consecutive concentric layer. This results in a higher total gravitational kinetic energy in any outside layer than the total gravitational kinetic energy in the next inner layer in any gravitational field. Thus, the first myth is resolved.

(c) **Gravitational attraction**

Gravitational attraction occurs due to the insufficient support that can be provided to both bodies by the common shared (solitary) space matrix in between. As a result, the bodies are pushed towards each other from all sides (see Figure 18).

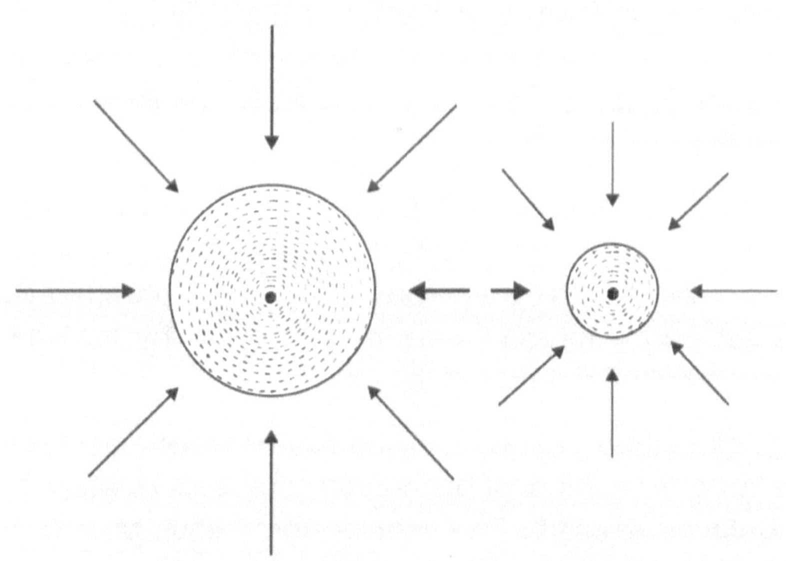

Figure 18 – Insufficient support from the common shared space matrix between the bodies causes them to fall towards each other.

Your second myth is that gravitational attraction is negative potential energy. The answer to this myth is that bodies fall or move towards each other because **the common shared space matrix**

cannot produce enough kinetic energy in between to support both bodies, leading to their fall or pushing towards each other.

However, it cannot be said, **that the deficient kinetic energy support to both bodies from in between is negative potential energy or gravity.**

(d) Proofs that Bodies behave as Weightless Point Masses

Newton stated that gravitation is the attraction between two bodies but he did not explain how or why this force is generated. Then Einstein proposed that it is produced by the deformation of omnipresent space-time. I have explained you above how gravitation works, which is to support a body by gravitational kinetic energy which is generated by proportionate contraction of space matrix to convert it into a symbolic weightless "point mass" on the space matrix.

First proof, all bodies, regardless of their size, big and small dropped from the Tower of Pisa by Galileo, came to the ground simultaneously because they were after being converted into weight less "point masses" were affected only by the same legendary gravitational field of the Earth.

Second, all planets orbit around the sun as weight less "point masses" at a "v" number of bound treos per second, where this speed determined only by their distance from the sun, and can be calculated by Newton's equation $MG=rv^2$, and independent of their individual masses, which are already neutralized by their own gravitational field.

(e) The unification of general theory with the quantum world; *'All big are many smalls'*

(A) GRAVITATIONAL WAVE, IS MULTIPLE MATTER WAVES

(i) **In the first and second dimensions the wave length reduces from S bound treos to just 1 bound treos with increasing quanta in a packet, reciprocally in third and fourth dimension wave length increases from 1 to S number** apex bound treos (S = 10^43) (Refer to Figure 23 in appendix).

(ii) In the gravitational field towards periphery when the kinetic energy goes on decreasing in the gravitational field with the dispersal of load on bigger layers from 4 th dimensional deformation in the gravitational sphere to 3 rd dimensional deformation in which the mass of the Sun accommodates and then in 2-dimensional deformation at 10^4 th quantum levels in the gravitational field of the sun in which planetary orbits forms this 10^39 frequency of matter wave (supporting 10^39 quanta mass in second dimension at 39 th quantum level in graviton coloumn) in the Earth's orbit with increasing frequency is again encountered in fourth dimension.

Same is kinetic energy and same layered kinetic coloumns i.e., same frequency of two waves (matter wave and gravitational wave); along with same two-dimensional deformations are in both fields which unites quantum world with general theory," or all Bigs are many smalls.

(B) Gravitational field of the sun (of 10^38-unit masses) is formed by merging of side-by-side placed 10^38 graviton coloumns (one for one unit mass) (figure 19)

(C) The gravitational sphere of sun is of 3 km diameter (2 x 10^38 graviton layers, equal to number of 10^38-unit masses which

constitutes Sun), the same is calculated by general theory and made up of many smalls of quantum world, by geometry in 'geometrical string Treo model'. (ref Blb.8)

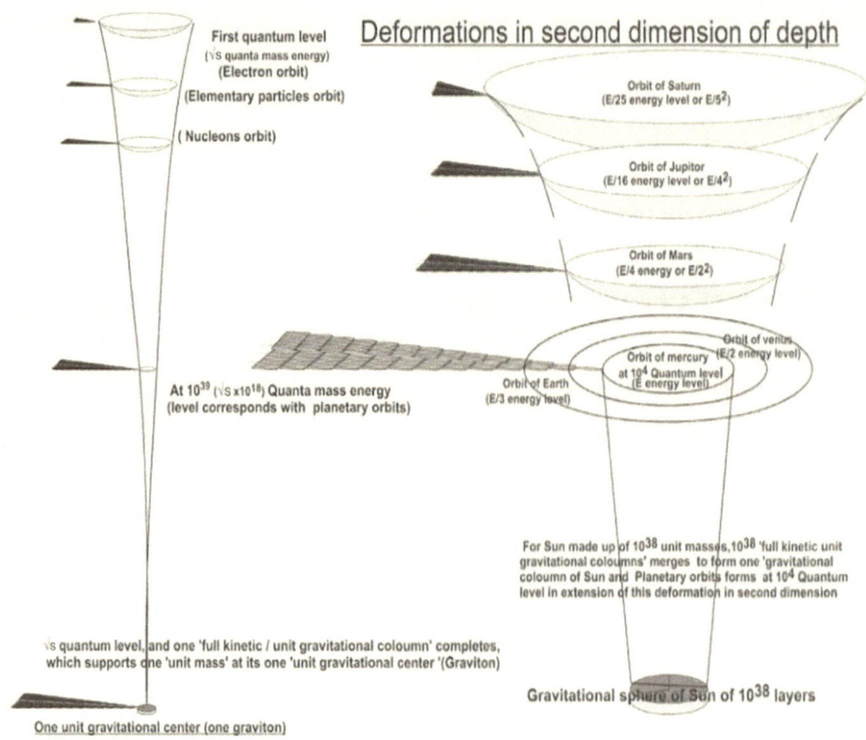

Figure 19 – Thus, as calculated and also proved by geometry, it comes out that, the gravitational field of the sun (of 10^38-unit masses body) is formed in one plane by merging of side-by-side placed 10^38 graviton coloumns (one for one unit mass). {While square number of Gravitons with their graviton coloumn in rotating kinetic coloumn of gravitational sphere (i.e., four-dimensional WAVE) are required to supports the exerted load of square of unit masses in Sun at its gravitational centre, to support it from all planes in one unit time of one second}.

(4) Atomic Fields and Gravitational Field Have Same Properties

1. *AT 137 times length of unit electron, in Bohr orbit, 137 th part of proton energy, exist as RH Rydberg's constant, and same is present in any orbit of any element.*

2. *The total energy in any atomic orbit is given by Rydberg's constant RH, which equals the 13.6 eV energy of the hydrogen atom, when calculated in joules, is 2.17×10^{-18} J, which is from 19.577×10^{64} Kinetons or treos (this is the proton energy 2.6×10^{67} treos, multiplied by the Fine Structure constant, 1/137). Rydberg's constant can also be expressed in terms of wave number, denoted as Rω.*

This RH energy, at the Bohr radius of 32.72×10^{23} bound treos, (equal to the wavelength of the electron in hydrogen atom 23.88×10^{21} bound treos, divided by the Fine Structure constant: 1/137), is not only in Bohr orbit of hydrogen but this supporting energy applies to any electron orbit in atoms of all elements.

As the atomic number increases at nucleus, the formula 2.17×10^{-18} J Z^2/n^2 (where Z is atomic number and n is quantum level) dictates that same uniform energy is present in any orbit of any element, and increasing *load in square* (Z^2) is supported by *square number of orbits* (n^2), which are formed at each next n th quantum level, results in uniform energy field which increases in periphery for bigger atoms of elements.

At four atomic quantum levels 1, 2, 3, and 4, (at which all elements form) the load is exerted in square of quantum level number in proportions of 1, 4, 9, and 16 times RH, which correspond to atomic energy levels K, L, M, and N. The increasing number of orbits are arranged in supporting shells formed: 1, 4, 9, 16, orbits within the subshells: *s, s p, s p d, and s p d f, at four quantum levels* with the one in *s* subshell at 1 Bohr radius, the three orbits are in *p* subshell at 4 Bohr radii, the five orbit in *d* subshell at 9 Bohr radii, and the seven orbit in *f* subshell at 16 Bohr radii as per coloumn geometry. The same RH energy is present in each orbit to support the exerted load, though the energy concentration in field remains same but the size of the field with increasing circumferences with distance. (Ref 170-180 Bib 8)

This concept is somewhat analogous to a gravitational field, where the **load 2M unit masses** exerted by a body of M unit masses on any layer in gravitational field remains constant. However, the energy concentration decreases, as the size reduces while the number of total supporting kinetic coloumns in subsequent bigger concentric layers increases. All kinetic coloumns together forms a gravitational wave that supports this fixed exerted load of 2M.

(f) FOUR BASIC FORCES or just one force in the universe

There is only one force in the universe, that increases proportionally to the load in an action-reaction mechanism. This force changes its geometry, nature, and magnitude as in contraction of matrix the number of dimensions of space-time increases. As a result, it manifests as the four different basic forces: the electromagnetic force, the atomic and weak forces, and the gravitational force.

These changing geometries forms all fields for all four basic forces, which are manifested as electro-weak fields, atomic energy fields, and gravitational kinetic energy fields and in gravitational fields.

Therefore, force is geometry. To understand what these four basic forces are, we need to study their changing geometries layer by layer at $\sqrt{S}$ quantum levels in each dimension. (Ref pages 100-149 in book BB 8).

Four forces are kinetic energy fields formed in response to applied load being supported by contraction an increasing number of dimensions with the increasing load.

Chapter 10

DAY 7

We discussed on 3 topics on this day with fellowing inferences.

(1) One Brane—Our Universe

Our universe is merely one brane within the vast multiverse, akin to a layer of an onion. This analogy explains why we perceive the universe as the surface of an inflating balloon (see Figure 20). Light enables us to visualize objects in one plane, creating two-dimensional images on this balloon-like surface. Consequently, we interpret our universe as "flat," with galaxies seemingly painted onto this expanded surface.

The Yajurveda 16/1 states

"ANANTKOTEBRAHMADNAYAKAY NAMAH," which means "I worship (Namah) God as the master (nayakay) of infinite (anantkote) universes (Brahmanda).

This highlights the Vedic advocacy for a multiverse concept.

Numerous mathematical models suggest the existence of parallel universes, collectively referred to as the multiverse, yet humanity remains distant from fully harnessing its potential. Despite their proximity, we remain oblivious to these parallel universes because our primary measurement tool, the telescope, is confined to the detection of light. As a result, the gravitational effects of nearby parallel universes that may cross the branes in between go unnoticed (Ref. *Universe in a Nutshell* by Stephen Hawking, 2001).

Alien explained, "consider the layers of an onion: your observed universe is just one layer among 26 total, according to string theory mathematics. Hawking refers to these layers as "branes." Although telescopes cannot reveal galaxies or solar systems from these alternate universes, we can perceive their gravitational effects. These forces arise from three- or four-dimensional deformations of the space matrix in parallel universes, occasionally penetrating the thin boundaries between universes.

Figure 20 – The Onion Peels Model of the Multiverse—A depiction of the multiverse, showing a common origin and end for all universes but with distinct "cosmic codes" for each brane of other universes.

Your body can perceive two natural forces: light and gravity. Through your eyes, you absorb photons (energy packets in the visible range of the electromagnetic spectrum) emitted by atoms. Through your middle ears, specifically the cochlea, you perceive gravitational forces, including balance and depth perception. When gravitational effects from black holes in neighboring universes occur, they may cause "pear-shaped" deformations in our universe's space matrix, potentially affecting Earth's atmosphere. If one of these deformations were to reach Earth, the consequences could be severe.

Our eyes only see what the brain knows. Unknown to most, as it's rarely discussed, gravitational effects from parallel universes are continuously present, which manifests as two-dimensional whirlpool deformations that may trigger tornadoes, especially in Oklahoma region of America, and can initiate processes to generate violent typhoons. In some cases, these three-dimensional gravitational columns—projected onto Earth by a four-dimensional deformation such as a 'black hole' from a neighboring universe—could even pull entire squadrons of planes or intact ships into them, to which we intercepted and re-directed to our labs, using our advanced technology. You can compare it with your doing experiments at Total Solar Eclipse."

I intercepted yes, I too remember an incidence about 30 years back in my life time when in clear weather a typhoon like weather suddenly struck the land in a 50 km straight belt from Prayagraj to New Delhi (580 km) which created such unknown tornado like gravitational pull in which even some cars were lifted and got hanged on trees.

At least 50 ships and 20 planes, including the USS *Cyclops* with 306 passengers in 1918, a squadron of five torpedo bombers (Flight 19) with 14 naval aviators in TBM Avengers in 1945, and all 13 crew members of the Martin PBM Mariner flying boat later launched to search for Flight 19, as well as the *Sulphur Queen* in 1963, vanished without a distress signal or trace of wreckage.

The Bermuda Triangle, located in the deepest North Atlantic Sea, bordered by Miami, Bermuda, and Puerto Rico, is known for erratic weather and magnetic disturbances. One survivor pilot reported his flying panel stopped working and with the formation of *electromagnetic froth* led his plane suck into a 'time-travel tunnel' in which his plane jumped by 100 km or so in no time (how it became possible please Refer (A) TIME TRAVEL section) while others reported hexagonal clouds and 'rough waves' producing two- and three-dimensional whirlpool deformations, generating 'waterspouts' or "tornadoes in the sea," in this region. The possibility of extraterrestrial forces cannot be ruled out as a cause of all of these events, as itself explained by Alien.

The South Atlantic Anomaly (SAA), a weak spot in the magnetosphere, can contribute to make this area vulnerable. Even the Hubble Telescope experiences electronic disruptions while passing over this area in South Atlantic ten times a day, making data collection impossible. Planes flying over this area are required to switch off all electronic devices, to save them from being permanent faulty.

Author adds that SAA may be due to the scientific fact of shifted Earth's magnetic center about 356 km from center of earth (due to Earth magnetic axis tilted to Earth rotational axis), resulting/ or resulted from shifting of Van Allen radiation belts; which contributes to 7% of earth magnetic field; over this area starting from 640 km and above up to 58000 km (with anomaly and a dip up to 200 km In this region – with elevation on opposite sides of globe) may be contributing its effects on 'Bermuda triangle' in west and 'Devils triangle' in east.

(2) The Lifespan of Our Universe: What proceeded the Big Bang

She said universe has a total lifespan of S seconds. During the 'unit time' of one second, each bound "Treo" vibrates in S directions of a circle, completing its S vibrations. To vibrate in all possible planes of a sphere (in all possible S circles on sphere), it takes S^2 vibrations in S seconds to complete the process. After this

---

FOOTNOTE:

This may the explanation as being valid claimed by the Alien for the mysterious disappearances in the Bermuda Triangle; as talked about previously also by some scientists on earth.

the universe's lifespan ends and also of the Treo life is exhausted, and by that time, the fully curled-up voids at big bang will uncurl completely due to the vibrational energy of adjacent Treos by its vibrations in all possible S^2 directions and all planes, in S^2 vibrations of S seconds. Then the five positive-dimensional Treos align with the five negative-dimensional equal sized voids after its full uncurling, they will inhale each other and the fabric of 10-dimensional space matrix will collapse instantly, resulting in a '**Big Crunch**' and matrix will re-convert in dense primordial soupe at its death in small area, but will not convert in singularity.

This will lead to sudden and violent contraction—the **Big Bang**—causes the "primordial soup" to recoil and form a new space matrix, starting the next lifespan of the universe. This ongoing slow expansion of universe by uncurling of voids drives the aging of everything within it, including both of us.

(3) Our Pendulum Universe

Our universe behaves like a quantum pendulum, oscillating between maximum kinetic energy state to maximum potential energy state as one swing of pendulum. At the moment of the Big Bang, the universe is in its maximum kinetic energy state, or fully contracted.

As it expands, it reaches to its maximum potential energy state, with a wrinkle-free space matrix, preparing for the inevitable Big Crunch or death of universe, just after full uncurling of voids. This process will take S seconds, or S^2 vibrations as one life span of universe.

The universe functions like a five-dimensional pendulum, with each "swing" representing one lifespan. This is similar to a wall clock's pendulum, along with Electromagnetic waves can also be viewed as a one-dimensional pendulum with crests and troughs, while planetary orbits, or electrons in elliptical paths, represent two-dimensional pendulums in the space matrix.

In essence, our universe is a five-dimensional pendulum system that swings between birth and death—between the Big Bang and the Big Crunch. Other universes in the multiverse experience similar cycles, collapsing at regular intervals. Despite having different cosmic codes and cosmic rhythm of vibrations, they all originated and will end at the same point with our universe.

Chapter 11

DAY 8 – PLANETS & THEIR POSITIONS

(1) You are from which planet, of which star?

Once I returned to my room at night, I was curious about the whereabouts of my alien companion, Grengi. I asked her, "You are from which planet, of which star?"

She answered, "I am from the star Gliese 581, which is in the constellation Libra." Being aware that Libra is my zodiac sign and having some interest in astronomy, I already knew the position of this star.

"And my planet is called E/4." I was perplexed by the peculiar name of her planet and wanted her to explain it. So, I said, "I could very well know about the position of your star, but I could not understand the strange name of your planet. Please explain it."

She replied, "I will explain your question by using the example of the positioning of the planets in your solar system." However, she first wanted to assess my knowledge of the positioning of celestial bodies in a gravitational field. I told her about my knowledge of Bode's relation, which relates to the position of bodies in the solar system.

She said, "Your knowledge is limited; 'Bode's relation' is only a rough approximation of the position of planets in the solar system, known to you. It does not explain the governing factors and the exact formula that can be used to determine the position of any baby bodies in the gravitational field of any parent body in the whole universe."

(2) What assigns the positions of baby bodies in any gravitational field?

Grengi, the alien, explained that planets in the solar system (comprising about 1% of material) condense at gravitational field quantum levels of our star (99% material SUN) in a two-dimensional deformation of any gravitational field of any parent body.

Stars form by the gravitational concentration of gas and ions present in a gaseous nebula. However, the space matrix regulates this accumulation of mass-energy, which should be incorporated into any 'simulation model of star formation.' The regulatory new factors should be added to the already known, are stated below:

1. **Disproportionate rise of value of -1 in 2n−1**: $2n-1$ kinetic columns in any layer of the gravitational field results in more TOTAL kinetic energy in any outer concentric layer than in the next inner layer, promoting the condensation of matter. Thus, matter is squeezed towards centre. (explained already as 'how the bodies move uphill'.)

2. In our quantum universe, energy accumulates only at the $\sqrt{S}$ quantum level in each dimension of the five dimensions of space-time-energy (For details, refer "$\sqrt{S}$ quantum level in each dimension" of this book chapter 7).

3. The resonance of all simultaneously vibrating all bound Treos (S number of times, in S directions of a circle, in S vibrations per second) regulates the geometry of the field and generates these quantum levels in any cosmic body at its resonance levels.

(3) Position of planetary quantum levels in any gravitational field

GRAVITATIONAL FIELD OF SUN

The Sun, composed of 10^38 unit masses, exerts a LOAD of (10^38)2 unit masses i.e., the square of unit masses which forms this body at its gravitational centre, and is supported by (10^38)2 gravitons in a 10^38 graviton layered gravitational sphere (kinetic column of the fourth dimension; 4 knots one over the other) around its gravitational centre.

The gravitational field *all around* is formed by merger of curled up graviton coloumns of (10^38)2 gravitons, forming the gravitational field of the Sun.

2×10^38 unit masses fixed LOAD is exerted on each layer in the gravitational field *in one plane* around its gravitational sphere, first it produces a 3-dimensional (3 knots) spherical deformation (matrix mould, in which the mass of the Sun in spherical shape accommodates) and then in 2-dimensional field the elliptical orbits form, in which all planets are located; the 1-dimensional deformation (1 knot field) present all around gravitational sphere serves as the plinth of the gravitational field (with increasing *Total Kinetic energy*, in each consecutive concentric bigger outer layer), and its geometry can be explained by Newton's field equations MG = rv^2 and MG = r^2a.

In any celestial cosmic body, smaller bodies (planets or natural satellites) start condensing primarily at the 10^4 th quantum level and extends up to the 10^5 th quantum level, with 10 planetary sub-quantum levels in between. This has been verified for satellites of the outer four planets and even calculated for planets of star Trappist outside our solar system (Refer to Bib 6). We will discuss how these planetary quantum levels are formed.

Formula for calculating the 10^4 th gravitational field quantum level' in any cosmic body:

Distance of any quantum level in bound Treo layers=(Square of quantum level)×(number of graviton layers in its gravitational sphere).

For example, for the Sun, the 10^4 th quantum level = (10^4)^2 multiplied by 10^38 layers in the gravitational sphere of the Sun = at radius of 10^46 layers in the gravitational field.

(4) Position of all planets at quantum levels

The expression V^2 represents the gravitational kinetic energy v^2 at any quantum level in each kinetic column at 2n−1 apex bound Treos in the wavelength of gravitational wave in this orbit, at n bound Treo layers (radius), together supporting total 2M unit masses Load (of M unit mass cosmic body). When this 2n−1 bound Treos wavelength of wave is multiplied by π (the value of PI), it calculates the circumference of this orbit.

If the gravitational kinetic energy level v^2, which can be calculated as (v^2=MG/r) in the orbit of the first planet Mercury, is E Kinetons, and the planet Mercury is in the first sub-shell of the shell at the *first planetary quantum level.*

FOOTNOTE:

<u>The geometry of formation quantum levels in Sun gravitational field:</u> The first gravitational field quantum level will be at (1) ^2 ×10^38 in the gravitational sphere of the Sun; the second will add 3 × 10^38 layers in gravitational field; the third will add 5×10^38 layers ; the fourth will add 10^38 layers, and so on …….It adds 2n−1 layers at any n th quantum level. This geometry gives the formula that any quantum level from the center can be calculated as the square of this quantum level number multiplied by the number of layers in the gravitational sphere of the Sun.

Then, (E/2) Kinetons will be present in each 'sub-kinetic column' in the orbit of Planet Venus, which is situated in the second sub-shell of the shell at the *first planetary quantum level.*

And (E/3) Kinetons will be in each 'sub-kinetic column' in the orbit of Planet Earth, placed in the third sub-shell of the shell at the *first planetary quantum level.*

E/4 or (E/2^2) Kinetons are in each sub-kinetic column in the orbit of Planet Mars.

So, my planet E/4E in my star corresponds to your planet, Mars.

E/9 or (E/3^2) Kinetons is the gravitational kinetic energy at the level of Asteroid belts,

E/16 or (E/4^2) Kinetons, in the orbit of Planet Jupiter, are present in each of 2n−1 kinetic coloumns, placed as one each at all apex bound Treos at n bound Treo radius from the Sun, which all together forms gravitational wave of Jupiter orbit.

E/25 or (E/5^2) Kinetons are in each kinetic column in the orbit of Planet Saturn,

E/49 or (E/7^2) Kinetons are in the orbit of Planet Uranus in all kinetic columns together forming a gravitational wave in orbit.

E/81 or (E/9^2) Kinetons are in the planetary orbit of Planet Neptune,

And E/100 or (E/10^2) exact Kinetons as gravitational kinetic energy v^2 are in the orbit of Planet Pluto.

(5) Revolution speed in any gravitational field

This kinetic energy v^2 at each point in an orbit decides the revolution or orbiting speed "v number of bound Treos per second" (which also equals the frequency of the gravitational wave and number of layers in kinetic coloumns in this orbit), by which the 'point mass' of the planet or any satellite of the outer planet will shift in one second in its orbit.

It is essential to note that the individual masses of planets are immaterial in deciding the orbital speed of a planet, as they are neutralized by their individual gravitational fields. Everything in the universe moves due to the local concentration of chromodynamic energy of the universe of the space matrix.

Thus, the moving Sun continuously deforms the local space matrix around it, moving at 792,000 km per hour with all planetary system, with the spinning galaxy; I.e., at 200 Km per second; while on top of it our galaxy is also moving at 2.1 million km per hour in the direction defined by the constellation Leo and Virgo towards the neighbouring galaxy Andromeda.

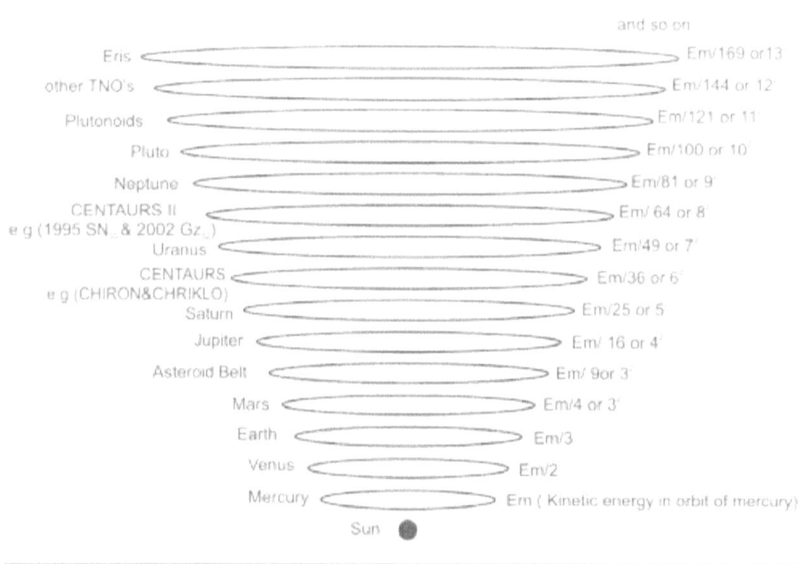

PLANETARY ORBITS (energy levels)

Figure 21 – Planets are placed at 10 'planetary quantum levels' formed in two-dimensional deformation of gravitational field of moving Sun

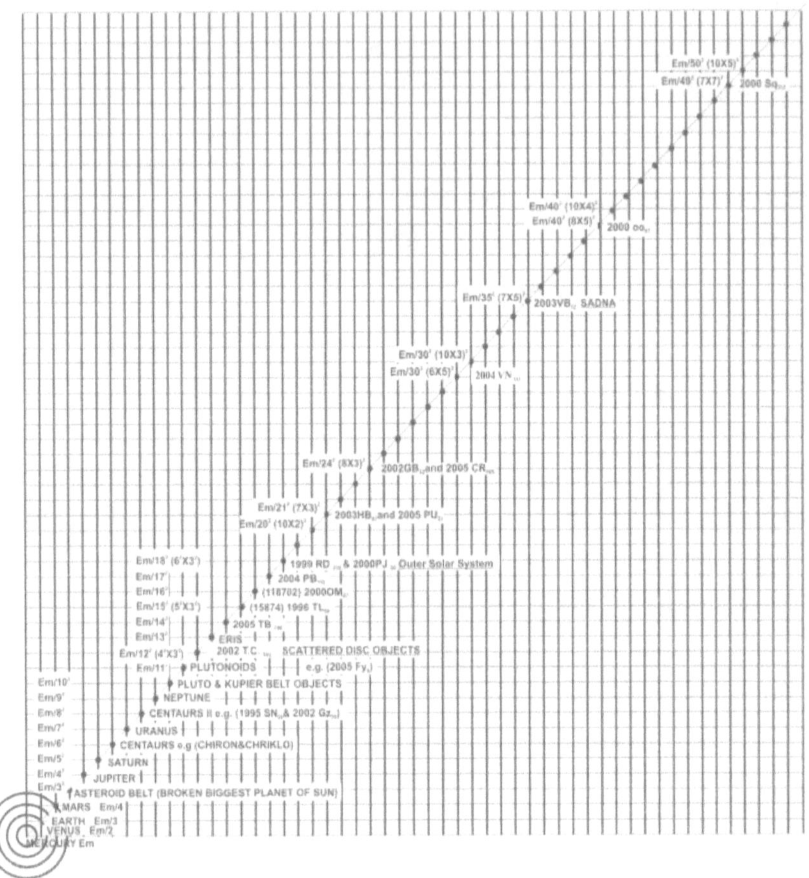

Energy level in the orbit of planets as calculated by the energy level in resept to the orbit of mercury

Figure 22 – Graph of gravitational kinetic energy 'v^2', in gravitational field of Sun, which also decides position of all baby bodies at quantum levels

About planetoids and 'Trans-Neptune objects' like one more planet Aries is at E/13^2 and far ahead in the 'outer solar system' planetoid Sudena is at E/35^2 are placed in 10^5th quantum level in gravitational field of Sun.

All planets discovered by the western world much later were described in Veda about 8000 years back (5600 BC) by their Vedic names. **Uranus** was called (ARYAMA), **Neptune** (VARUN),

Pluto (RITU) in Rigveda (1/105/6). The Vedas names Ring of Saturn and divides them in 3 parts, as Shukra, Suchaya, and Ruchanaha (Rigveda 4/51/9).

(6) Configuration of planets

Not only is space deformed by the presence of matter, but reciprocally the properties of space (along with the kinetic energy level) around cosmic bodies affect and shape the configuration (state of matter, i.e., solid, liquid, or gaseous).

The concentration of gravitational kinetic energy v^2 at its quantum level in local space matrix decides the density of all solid planets in any gravitational field.

Thus, 'gaseous outer planets in the solar system' have satellites that have solid bodies

As my mother planet is at "E/4 of star cirrus (just as copy of your star, the Sun)," it is in a position equivalent to E/4 or the planet Mars in your solar system, and that is why the density of the body mass of my planet at E/4 is slightly less than the density of your planet Earth, which is placed in a higher density gravitational kinetic energy orbit (E/3), i.e., in side more deformed space matrix around it.

That is why you live for 100 years and we live 1000 years due to initial coding present in our genes (formed in womb) and we born in different kinetic energy zones. The birth of babies in different constellations in different months of year provides them distinct brains and mental capacities, properties, nature, behaviour which is unique for the child born in particular month, as the gravitational kinetic energy of legend gravitational field of sun around earth varies due to different location of planets around sun (and around Earth).

Thus, formed PAN CHANG (in 57 BC by king Vikramaditya) which started 'Hindu Calander' still used in Hindu science of living (Sanatana dharma), to predict about life of all children's born in the, form of "Janam Patri" prepared, according at which particular time (second in year) child born, later adopted in culture of China. While performing marriage of this child its "Janam Patri" will be matched with "Janam Patri" of Girl in arranged marriages system in Hindus which follow Sanatan science of living.

Like other religions, Sanatan dharma in no religion, but it Is Sanatan science of living, which has its roots in Vedas (5600BC) and not related with any incarnation Ram or Krishna (as all religions are related with some legendary figures as incarnation) all created and distorted by MYTHOLOGY, for benefits of some strong, still being cashed by governments all around world, as ever been cashed by kings and priests, in human history on your planet EARTH, to befool the masses, main plight of you earthlings.

(7) It was biggest planet which exploded

The Alien revealed one more fascinating truth about the planetary system of the Sun.

She said "your solar system has quite a violent history. The 'Asteroid belts' are the remains of the broken pieces of the biggest planet of the solar system."

I said, I may agree with you that the remains of an exploded planet formed an asteroid belt, but how can you say that the planet which exploded was the 'biggest planet of the solar system'?

I will give you one circumstantial mathematical proof: the asteroid belts are at **v2/3^2 (i.e., at E/9), and this is the position fixed for the 'biggest baby body' in any gravitational field.**

Examples are, the biggest satellite of Jupiter, Ganymede (Diameter 5262 km), is situated at the kinetic energy level of E/9 (while E is the kinetic energy level of the first satellite of Jupiter). The biggest satellite of Saturn, Titan (Diameter 5150 km), the biggest satellite of Uranus, Titania (Diameter 1578 km), the biggest satellite of Neptune, Triton (Diameter 2706 km) all are at the kinetic energy level E/9 at the quantum level in their respective gravitational fields.

Thus, we can safely conclude that the biggest planet of the Sun must have existed at this quantum level in the solar gravitational field at E mercury/9, kinetic energy level.

A significant part of the debris of the exploded planet of Sun was embedded in the baby Moon (Earth's sole satellite) in its early life, which resulted in he uneven density of the moon'.

Chapter 12

DAY 9

I asked Grengi to tell me what love is. She said, "Love is quantum entanglement of two souls, which reflects to us the picture of God. Let us discuss something else today, I will explain about love some other time."

(A) How Do You Perceive?

I inquired how she could see, hear, feel, and even know my thoughts. She replied, "Today I'll explain the workings of my body and the advanced technologies involved with this helmet. In our galaxy, the advancement of any civilized species is measured by how much they understand the space-matrix (which you might refer to as our 'regulatory god') and how that knowledge is applied to their technology. You, along with all the scientists who have ever lived, have only scratched the surface by exploring isolated properties of this matrix."

(B) How Do You See?

I asked her, "If a photon is just a packet of different numbers of EM energy quanta, how can you see around all colors?"

She explained, "Every atom in the universe absorbs EM energy from incident photons of fixed quanta energy i.e., frequency, exciting its electrons, which shift to a higher quantum level. The released photon made up of different quanta energy and frequency unique to that element or compound, as the difference in concentration of EM energy at two quantum levels differs in each element or compound.

When the excited electron in an atom returns to its baseline, it releases a photon with energy corresponding to the difference in energy concentration between the two subshells. The extent of the jump of the electron between subshells determines the type of photon released (i.e., *the more you pull the catapult the bigger the stone you can throw*). The type of photon absorbed and released is fixed for the element. By analyzing dark lines in the spectrometry of light received from any star, we know the absorbed photon energy by any element, while the white lines represent the released EM energy from that element. Thus, by such **signatures of elements**, we can identify elements and their presence on distant stars, many light-years away.

The electromagnetic spectrum, which includes radio waves, microwaves, infrared, visible light, ultraviolet, X-rays, and gamma rays, consists of photons having integral multiples of one quantum of EM energy, which totals $\sqrt{S}$ *types of photons formed at* $\sqrt{S}$ *quantum levels of first dimension*. Each photon packet in the EM spectrum generates EM waves of increasing frequency equal to the EM energy quanta in the packet. You perceive colors by absorbing different quanta of EM energy from photons in the visible spectrum (wavelengths between 400nm and 700nm). When these photons hit your retina, the EM energy is sent to the visual cortex at the back of your brain."

She continued, "This energy of photons or excitons is absorbed by our brains, allowing us to see and identify colors according to the type of photon—the size of the energy stone absorbed by the retina."

That night, with only the lamp on my computer desk illuminating the room, I noticed something odd: I was casting a shadow, but the alien's shadow was absent. I turned to her and asked, "What happened to your shadow?" Suddenly, I couldn't see her at all.

"I'm still here," she said. "I'm demonstrating that you can't see me because I can become invisible at will."

Surprised, I could only utter, "How?"

She replied, "First, let me explain how you cast shadows. The atoms of all elements absorb photons of particular frequencies when exposed to light, and our bodies, made up of many elements, absorb or reflect sunlight, casting shadows. The changed refractive index of different tissues from skin down, makes your body opaque.

You've seen me—I have no eyes—but I absorb photon packets across the total surface of my skull. My entire skull functions like your retina, enabling me to analyze my surroundings in 360 degrees. This is how I sensed you before you fell into the ice crater and caught you, saving your life.

I also absorb light and other EM spectra as an energy source for our body, to carry out biochemical processes, and to maintain our fixed body temperature. Absorbing the full EM spectrum is essential for our survival, similar to plants on Earth, which use photon energy in photosynthesis to create carbohydrates from water and carbon dioxide and for other uses as temperature sensitivity.

1. We even use absorbed EM energy to directly power our brains, making our bodies highly efficient in energy utilization.

2. When we're hungry, starving for energy, our defensive mechanism can even voluntarily stop emitting photons of any frequency from the atoms in our skin. This makes us invisible to others at night. This effect can be compared to 'total internal reflection of a black body.'

3. We can also become transparent. Light bends while passing through materials with different refractive indices,

which usually makes tissues opaque. This is how a pencil appears bent when placed in a glass of water. However, when all the tissues in our body have the same refractive index, we can become transparent and we aliens can do it with our will. Thus, we will not generate any shadow of our body.

We can also camouflage our bodies by emitting photons so that our bodies perfectly match the surroundings, much like some fishes whose colors match those of the sea floor."

(C) My Helmet (and Telepathy)

"Thoughts are generated with the emission of photons during quantum-level jumps of circulating electrons in your cerebral cortex. These excited electrons, called excitons, reflect to your consciousness.

The receiver of this helmet receives input (similar to the working of your brain) by analyzing unique wavelengths in the beams of these emitted photons, which are responsible for your various thoughts. Thoughts are associated with the formation of kinetic coloumns (wrinkles) along the wavelengths of each photon on the space matrix, quantum entangled with the beam of the soul (electrons).

Simultaneously, while absorbing the beams of photons, the helmet receiver (through a brain-computer interface) conducts EEG (the electroencephalogram of your brain). The inbuilt quantum computers first filter out some known wavelengths produced by all signals required to operate the body functions of your vital organs, as well as some artifacts. Then they analyze the wavelengths of the remaining signals (produced by your brain, which, in turn, operates your vocal cords to generate different patterns of voices). Thus, we can directly know your thoughts, your language, and the content of your speech.

Now you know how we achieve mental telepathy. The kilometers-long deformation of the matrix produced by your thought photons can be perceived not only by this helmet and our sophisticated gadgets but even directly by any tuned receiver brain. You might call it telepathy."

(D) Superluminal Speeds

"How does your spaceship travel faster than the speed of light in this universe, breaking the speed limit barrier—the speed of light, the ultimate fixed limit of motion in the universe?" I asked.

She replied, "We use three methods to achieve superluminal speeds.

1. Travel in Higher Dimensions:

"Planets and satellites move in their orbits (by v^2 gravitational kinetic energy in orbit) to move at v bound Treo distance per second in a gravitational field. Similarly, S^2 kinetons, as base energy in the space matrix, provide S bound treos per second speed to photon packets, which is the speed of light.

Imagine a travellator at a railway station—you can move faster than its base speed by walking or running on a travellator that is moving at its base speed. To move in higher-dimensional deformation, our engines eject neutron beams at subluminal speeds, which orbit around our spaceship, **creating artificial moving spaces in higher dimensions**.

For your information, the pyramids, with their enormous weight, are built to create three-dimensional deformation in the central chamber where the pharaoh's body is kept, generating a space of high energy concentration in the local deformed matrix in higher dimensions. Thus, we create three-dimensional local deformations that concentrate maximum S^3 kinetons (or

S number of gravitons) as its base energy at each point of this higher dimension, providing additional kinetic energy to our spaceship to **generate a bigger baseline push along its path.**

2. Space Contraction:

Not only does it generate a higher push, but "the 'carpet' of space between us and our destination rolls up in higher dimensions, effectively reducing the distance we need to travel.

Not only does time slow down, but space also contracts with artificially increased kinetic energy levels due to the interdependence of its three components of space, time, and energy.

This allows our spaceship to take great leaps of space-time (what happens in the Bermuda Triangle; please refer to footnote at page 115). By traveling through higher dimensions, we gain energy boosts and **shorten the road to our destination**.

3. Multiverse Travel:

We usually travel through multiverses to reach distant regions of this universe quickly, by navigating through other branes of the multiverse (other universes), much like traveling through a wormhole or an underground metro system that offers shortcuts. To enter a parallel universe, our spaceship adjusts to the different universal constants of that universe, which are governed by its unique 'cosmic code', based on the rhythm of its cosmic vibrations.

You may have seen UFOs suddenly disappear from view. They're entering a parallel universe with slightly different values of their universal constants, to which our spaceship adjusts. This helps us travel via wormholes or shortcuts to distant destinations much faster. For instance, I travelled from my planet, 600 light-years away, to yours in less than three weeks."

(E) Different Lifespans of Species

At that moment, my female dog entered the room. She started barking at the sight of the alien, who observed her with interest and asked two questions simultaneously. "What is your lifespan, and what is the lifespan of this dog on Earth?"

I replied, "We live for about 100 years, while dogs live for around 15 years. Some insects, on the other hand, live for just a day on Earth. But, why is that?"

"Every species can exist within its specific quantum levels, determined by their genomes. The contraction of the space matrix not only supports different loads, but the characteristics of the locally contracted space matrix also affect our life spans," said see.

"The space matrix—space, time, and energy—has three interdependent components. When one of these components' changes, the other two adjust. When space contracts, kinetic energy erupts, and local time slows down," she continued.

"As I mentioned earlier, the universe constantly readjusts and expands slightly in each Planck's least time interval—the smallest possible unit of time. The reaction to an action doesn't happen instantaneously; it takes at least one Planck time to react. This is what we call 'processing time' or 'reaction time'—the minimum time required for change".

"This ongoing adjustment in the universe, through local contractions of space and the expansion of its voids, is what you perceive as the 'flow of time.' All biochemical processes rely on this 'processing time,' and the lifespan of any species is directly tied to the speed of this processes going on within their bodies.

"As the gravitational field of Sun strengthens toward its core, the flow of time slows down relative to the contraction of the local space matrix, at each **next quantum level.**

"For example, a dog's foetus matures in just two months, while a human takes nine months, and an elephant takes two years. **The different rates of biochemical processing determine these differences**".

"A housefly can flap its wings 600 times per second and lives its entire lifespan in just one day, perceiving that short span as we perceive in our 100-year lifespan.

"On my planet, located one quantum level above yours, the average lifespan is around 1000 years. If you were to live on my planet, you would also live for another 900 years."

Chapter 13

DAY 10 – PURPOSE IN THE UNIVERSE

"Purpose is always at the core of the workings of the universe. Everything happens to serve the creator's purpose, which in turn makes the universe conscious and offers proof of HIS invisible and omnipresent existence.

Let me explain you with an example: What could have been the purpose of gravitation? How can you explain, you only know gravitation as force of attraction in between two bodies, you are ignorant about How it is produced. But I already told you HOW it is produced, but now I will tell WHY it is at all generates. You can visualize it as old lady gathering matter from all around and crushing in in her hand driven 'two stones grinder'.

(!) Purpose of Gravitational Force in the Universe

Our universe is expanding, but why is the rate of expansion is accelerating? Gravity plays a crucial role by the churning of all matter in ever increasing amount; it makes the space matrix wrinkle-free and thus contributes to its expansion. If the void causes expansion of the sheet of space matrix, gravity presses it out, removing its wrinkles to accelerate the expansion (crude analogy, as electric iron presses your shirt to make it wrinkle free).

All matter is gathered by gravity to form larger bodies, and then gravitational spheres and black holes churn this matter, resulting in Hawking radiation that releases positive energy particles (TREOS) and negative energy as voids. **Smaller the gravitational sphere (black hole in formation), more it churns.** The negative energy is reabsorbed by these bodies, while positive energy, exemplified by the Sun, is released from a 3 km diameter gravitational sphere of the Sun through this churning of matter. This energy facilitates the flow of solar wind and serves as the driving force behind it as "ENERGY RESPONSIBLE FOR FLOW OF CHARGED PARTICLES IN SOLAR WIND".

For comparison, the Earth's gravitational sphere (black hole in formation) which measures only 1 mm i.e., 10^{32} graviton layers, helps to heat the Earth's core, move tectonic plates, and cause volcanic eruptions through the energy released. (for comparison, Sun has gravitational sphere of 3 Km diameter is of 10^{38} graviton layers, while gravitational sphere of unit black hole, in 3 lac km diameter and have 10^{43} graviton layers). These layers in gravitational sphere are always equal to the number of Unit masses which form this body.

This churning of matter is essential for removing all wrinkles (the open knots tied one over the other, which can form up to five knots in the space matrix—like five Russian dolls, one inside the other). This process aims to flatten and smooth the space matrix, preparing it for the Big Crunch, or the death of the universe—total disintegration of the matrix architecture by the engulfing of all TREOS (after consuming all energy of S^2 vibrations in S seconds) by all voids. The collapse of the whole matrix will happen instantaneously, bouncing back in a Big Bang, creating a contracted ball that will be born as a new universe. Thus, one swing of our quantum pendulum universe represents one lifespan of our quantum pendulum universe, totalling S seconds.

The constant expansion of the matrix not only causes the expansion of the universe but also leads to the expansion of chromosomes present in every cell of our DNA i.e. Genome, responsible for our aging and that of all creatures. This can be identified by the gradual decrease in the number of wrinkles on the corners of all chromosomes since birth.

(!!) My Purpose of Being in the Universe

On the 10th day, I found myself contemplating whether we were alone in the universe, whether aliens truly existed, or if everything I had experienced was just a dream or an illusion. I began to believe that everything in the universe occurs for a hidden purpose, and this purpose serves as proof of a conscious universe, guiding and influencing events.

As I reflected on this, I started to see a deeper meaning in my encounter with the alien and was reminded of a significant incident from my past.

Let me take you back about 50 years, to the year 1973, when I was doing my one-year house residency after passing my MBBS. During this time, I experienced an emotional upheaval. Having struggled with asthma since childhood, I often suffered from severe bronchial spasms that left me breathless. A couple of times, I even experienced "status asthmaticus," a life-threatening condition. During my residency, I resolved to address this issue before leaving medical college. The only treatable physical cause for my asthma was a deviated nasal septum (DNS), so I sought help from Dr. U.K. Mishra, a lecturer in the E.N.T. department, to perform the DNS operation. Despite his polio-related gait, Dr. Mishra was a skilled surgeon. He advised me to undergo pre-operative investigations, including a chest X-ray.

When Dr. Trehan, a lecturer in the radiology department, examined my X-ray, he discovered a 3 cm by 3 cm "cannonball shadow" in the upper lobe of my left lung. Concerned, a bronchoscopy biopsy was recommended, and Dr. R.C. Tandon, a new cardiothoracic lecturer fresh from the U.S., was eager to perform it. A classmate of mine, Dr. Shakya, who was pursuing a diploma in anaesthesia, administered the anaesthesia. He later told me that I turned blue on the operating table due to oxygen deprivation, forcing him to ask the surgeon to stop the procedure. Unfortunately, the biopsy was unsuccessful.

Recently, Dr. Rajesh Bhargav, my batchmate and now a professor of surgery, reminded me that I had been working as Dr. Tandon's house resident at the time. I not only turned blue but Dr. Tandon himself had to perform CPR (cardiopulmonary resuscitation) on me when my heart stopped after the procedure.

The following day, after a discussion among Dr. Tandon, Dr. Mishra, Dr. Trehan, and Dr. A.P. Mathur (a resident radiologist), Dr. Mathur informed me that, without a successful biopsy, they collectively diagnosed the shadow as lymphosarcoma, a type of malignant tumor.

I asked him how long I had to live. With a solemn expression, he told me the prognosis was grim—no more than six months. I asked if it could be treated anywhere in India, and he replied that there were no treatments available for this cancer within the country. With no money and no support to seek treatment abroad, I was left with little hope.

At the time, the film *Anand* was playing at Agra's Chitra cinema. In the movie, the protagonist, Anand, was suffering from lymphosarcoma of the intestine. Viewers empathized with him, admiring his philosophy of life and death as he shared heartfelt dialogues with his friend, Babu Moushai. The film was a big hit, and now I found myself living a version of Anand's story.

After my diagnosis, I kept the news to myself, not sharing it with my friends or family. I continued my duties, despite the heavy workload of patients at the medical college in Agra. My father had passed away two years prior, at the age of 51. My younger brother, Yogesh, was a 20-year-old law student, and my 16-year-old sister, Archana, was still in intermediate college. My mother was a housewife, and my house resident stipend of Rs. 350 per month was the only small income of my entire family. Burdened with financial responsibilities and consumed by fear, I remained silent, showing no sign of my inner turmoil to anybody.

With no hope for the future, I took out a life insurance policy for Rs. 20,000, knowing that I could at least afford the premiums from my modest earnings and this will pull my family after me for some time.

The next month, I went for another chest X-ray. The tumor was still there, unchanged. The same result followed in the second, third, and fourth months. However, during the fifth month, as I was waiting for my X-ray, something extraordinary happened. A bright light enveloped me, and I heard a clear voice say, "You are being held back for important tasks that you must accomplish."

When I saw my X-ray a few hours later, everyone, including myself, was astonished. The tumor was gone. There was no longer any "cannonball" shadow in my lung. I had been miraculously cured.

It was at this moment that the alien burst into laughter, revealing that it was she who had eradicated all my cancer cells with a laser beam burst while remaining invisible. The helmet I wore echoed back, "My love for you and humanity is not insignificant or cheap. As a token of my love, I will take you to my planet, where we can live happily for another 900 years or so," Then we planned for my possible extradition to her planet.

FOOTNOTE:

Perhaps the purpose of my life was simply to share this divine knowledge of our working god—the chromodynamic energy named the universe—for the benefit of humanity before migrating to the alien's planet. I am leaving behind this text as 'papers in the printer bucket' (from chapter 3 to chapter 13), which may serve as 'Theory of everything".

Chapter 14

THE FINAL PAGE

Written on August 15, 2024

It was finally time to reveal everything. That's why, for the first time since Grengi's death, I unlocked the closed room on the first floor of my house in the early hours of the night on August 15th, 2024— the very room which I locked myself permanently on the day of Grengi's sacrifice, about eleven years earlier.

Inside, I searched for the printouts, the record of my discussion with the alien. They had been lying in the printer tray all these years. I found them untouched, exactly as they had been. I have included them in this book (as chapters 3 through 13).

I also found the crucial instructions I had left on the computer screen for my son, Ashwarya, written 11 years ago. I have included them too (as chapter 2).

On that morning of 15 th August 2013 Ashwarya had wisely followed my instructions. He did not cremate my body, as I had requested, waiting until September 5th, 2013. He also kept secret the fact that I had somehow come back to life after being in a state of 'suspended animation' for 21 days.

To my astonishment, I discovered that the helmet I had placed on a stool beside my bed, near the alien papers, had turned to ashes along with the alien papers and its 3 lectures. There was no proof left of the alien's existence.

On that fateful night, exactly 11 years ago, on August 15th, 2013, I had been granted provisional permission from the Alien

Council to be transported to their planet, with only the final signature from the Masters of the Universe pending. My soul began its journey on a spaceship with my alien friend, as we had planned.

However, after 10 days of travel through space, my alien friend received devastating news: the permission to transport a human soul and then to reassemble the body on their planet had been denied by the Master of the Galaxy. She was ordered to abandon my soul in space and return to her planet.

Grengi, outraged by this decision, rebelled. She ordered the robots on the spaceship to reverse course and return to Earth, severing all communications of her space craft with her home planet. She knew the space ship had just enough nuclear fuel for a round trip, but she was determined.

When she reached Earth after 10 more days, the spaceship hovered above my house in the dead of night. Grengi, using a rope attached to her transparent astronaut suit, descended onto my open roof in front of my room, with my soul jar and the halo camera. She detached herself from the rope, entered my room, and, after removing and coupling and readjusting the helmet which was still on my skull, with her halo matrix camera, she re-introduced my soul into my body. My soul, like a magnet drawn to its iron cage i.e. my brain, got attached to my body which was in 'suspended animation'. It was around 3 AM, on that action full night of September 4th and 5th, 2013.

After reviving me, Grengi told me everything that had happened since she collected my soul on the Independence Day of 2013. 20 days before our space journey.

In gratitude, I kissed her skull for the first time. She reciprocated with a soft sound in my helmet.

Grengi then asked me to leave the room, and come out, while still wearing the helmet. As she gathered up the halo camera and the now-empty soul jar, she instructed me to watch her spaceship as it ascended. She reattached herself to the cord and soon returned to the still-hovering craft, about 15 metres above.

As the ship rose just half a kilometre into the sky, my helmet echoed her final words: "Dearest, after I rebelled, I had no choice left. Your revival was a must and my duty to pass this knowledge to all, for the benefit of all humanity, as it will change the course of science. I've just pressed the suicide button on my spaceship. It will activate in one minute, giving me time to reconsider. But, at this last minute, as I've already programmed your helmet and the spaceship's instruments to merge my soul with your soul as soon as I die, and thus I will energise your body and soul for the rest of your life. After its merger, your soul will take a quantum leap to bliss, or even higher.

You once asked me what love is—now I can only say, my love for you, and for humanity, was never cheap. Good luck and goodbye.........

Those were the last words I could hear before a massive jolt hit me. In a flash of light, I saw her spaceship explode and disintegrate. Then I passed out.

I don't know how long I was unconscious that night, but when I awoke, the helmet echoed her remaining last sentence to me, spoken as I lost consciousness: ....this knowledge is for all; this is what you must know before you die."

Completely broken inside, I placed the helmet on the side stool next to Grengi's papers. I locked the room and went downstairs, where, as usual, breakfast was being prepared.

Since then, I never gone upstairs to my room till this day, meanwhile in last 11 years I wrote 4 books and published few papers all mentioned in the bibliography of this book, and thus I could carve long awaited this **THEORY OF EVERYTHING** and could repay her gratitude.

May our sleeping humanity will wake up to take a big step ahead, with the help of this virgin alien knowledge, passed only second time to us, after SHRUTI, or so called four books of Vedas spoken, by so called such Gods.

FOOTNOTE:

"that is what you must know before you DIE" kept on haunting me. As she said and honouring her sacrifice, it is kind duty of every reader is to further spread this knowledge to fulfil her last wish 'we all owe her at least this, in exchange of knowledge she boosted to all Human race.'

APPENDIX A

CALCULATIONS

(A) Reduced Planck's constant and Planck constant

One quantum of energy or S number of treos is the value of the Reduced Planck constant, ℏ bar. It produces a unit action and deforms just one bound Treo layer of the unit space matrix, along with its one 'unit angular momentum' (value of h; Planck constant), which produces one electromagnetic wave in one second.

Reduced Planck's Constant (ℏ):

The Reduced Planck constant, ℏ (also known as h bar), represents one quantum of energy and is given by:

ℏ=1.0545718×10^-34 Joule second (CO-DATA 2018 value)

It defines the unit action and deforms one bound Treo layer of the unit space matrix. The value of the Planck constant h is:

h=6.626070×10^-34 Joule second (CO-DATA 2018 value)

Relationship:

ℏ= h divided by 2π = 6.626070×10−34 divided by 6.28318531 =1.05457179×10^−34 Joule second

Mass of One Quantum of Energy:

If we calculate the mass of this energy (m = E / c^2): 1.05457179 × 10^-34 Joule / (2.99792458 × 10^8 metres per second) ^2 = 1.17336936 × 10^-51 kg (mass of one quantum of energy).

(B) Speed of Light

Each time, after one Planck's least time, by the next vibration, the photon packet slides in translational motion to the adjoining 'next bound Treo' in the direction of its progression on the space matrix. Thus, by S vibrations in one second, it moves a distance of S number (i.e., $1.855394405 \times 10^{43}$) of bound treos per second. The speed of light = Number of vibrations per second × displacement of the photon packet per vibration.

$= (1.855394409 \times 10^{43})$ vibrations per second × $(1.615788303 \times 10^{-35})$ m = 2.997924×10^{8} metres per second, which is c, or the speed of light in a vacuum. Hence,

$c = S \cdot LP$

*Where Planck's least length or LP = $1.615788303 \times 10^{-35}$m is the space occupied by one bound Treo in length.

(C) Recalculated Derived Value of the Gravitational Constant

The new derived value of the gravitational constant (to know what it denotes) can be calculated by replacing the metre with Planck's least length.

The gravitational constant, **"G," is 6.67430×10^{-11} metre ^{3} per kilogram per second per second.** (dimensional formula L3 M-1 T-2).

"G" can be recalculated in terms of bound treos (kinetons) by substituting the value of the metre with the natural unit of Planck's least length, which is the size of one bound Treo (**1 metre = $0.61871425 \times 10^{35}$ bound treos**).

G = $6.67430 \times 10^{-11} \times (0.61871425 \times 10^{35})$ ^{3} bound treos (kinetons) per kilogram per second per second

= 1.58079692 × 10^94 kinetons per kilogram per second per second.

This also means that this number of kinetons acts on 1 kilogram of mass per second per second and will support an equal number of "Treos" in one kilogram. Thus, 1.58079692 × 10^94 "Treos" constitute one kilogram of mass.

Alternatively, the value of "G" can also be denoted by the number of kinetons supporting one unit of mass (S^2 number of Treos = 3.442488398 × 10^86 treos) as **= 3.442488398 × 10^86 kinetons per unit mass, per second per second.**

+Alternatively, the value of "G" can also be denoted by the number of kinetons acting on one free Treo (as seen in the case of EM wave of unit photon) and **= 1 kineton per free Treo, per second per second.**

Then, gravitation as a phenomenon can be explained as G a universal constant = 1 unit action by one free Treo is reacted by one kineton by its one-unit reaction, each time which completes in one unit time of 1 second, i.e., per second per second (i.e., continuously).

(D) What condenses mass in bodies, and gives slope towards body?

What condenses mass of cosmic body and pushes/squeezes the baby body towards the centre of the mother body in any gravitational field, despite bigger sub-kinetic columns and dense kinetic energy towards the centre?

Gravitational condensation in a cosmic body occurs due to the **decreasing total gravitational kinetic energy per layer as we approach the centre of the body.** The formula:

$2MG \geq (2n-1) \times v2$

As in this equation the value of the factor -1 increases disproportionately fast,

thus, it results in that the total gravitational kinetic energy in one-layer decreases in each successive layer towards the centre. This reduction provides a gentle slope causing bodies to move towards the centre of the gravitational field.

While the gravitational kinetic energy (v^2) of each sub-kinetic column in each successive layer towards the sun increases, the total gravitational kinetic energy of any one n th layer on 2n-1 kinetic columns does not stay constant but comparatively reduces fast in each successive layer (matter wave) towards the sun, as the value of the factor -1 increases disproportionately fast. This happens with decreasing value of 'n' (as 'n' is also equal to the radius or distance from the sun) in the equation [$2MG \geq (2n - 1) \times v^2$]. The impact of the -1 factor increases disproportionately fast as 'n' approaches 1, towards the gravitational centre of the body. $2MG \geq (2n - 1) \times v^2 \geq MG$ ('r' or 'n' is large and 1 is small)

In each successive layer towards the sun, the value of 2MG kinetons (i.e., the total gravitational kinetic energy in one layer) is calculated to be less than in the next outer layer according to the formula $2MG \geq (2n - 1) v^2$. For example, see one hypothetical calculation of "total kinetic energy in one layer" from layer number 1 to layer number 10 in a gravitational field, which is calculated as 1 MG, 1.5 MG, 1.66 MG, 1.75 MG, 1.80 MG, 1.83 MG, 1.85 MG, 1.87 MG, 1.88 MG, and 1.9 MG. This anomaly provides a gentle slope towards the parent body, and thus, the body mass and baby bodies in the gravitational field will slide/fall/squeeze towards the sun due to the total pushing force of one full outer bigger layer.

(E) Planets condense at matching 'gravitational kinetic energy (v^2) level'

Calculation of Gravitational Kinetic Energy in the Orbit of Mercury as E is equal to the total number of kinetons (v^2) in any one 'sub-kinetic column' at which the planetary orbit of our first planet Mercury lies (according to the formula E = v^2 = MG/r).

Gravitational Kinetic Energy in Planetary Orbit of Mercury

The gravitational kinetic energy v^2 or E for Mercury:

E =8.776444393×10^78 kinetons

Calculated as: (V^2 = MG/ r)

E= 3.145233887×10^124 (MG); divided by 0.3583722239×10^46 ('r ')

Gravitational kinetic energy or v^2 in the orbit of any planet determines its position at its matching 'planetary quantum level'.

(F) Planetary Orbits are placed at kinetic energy quantum levels

Kinetic energy values for planets compared with theoretical values:

Planet	Calculated E	Actual E
Mercury	8.776444393×10^78.	8.776444393×10^78.
Venus	4.38822197×10^78	4.696829258×10^78
Earth	2.925481464×10^78	3.397352232×10^78
Mars	2.194111098×10^78	2.230118005×10^78
Asteroid belt	0.975160488×10^78	
Jupiter	0.548527774×10^78	0.653301797×10^78
Saturn	0.351057775×10^78	0.356398183×10^78

Planet	Calculated E	Actual E
Uranus	0.1791111×10^78	0.177026782×10^78
+Neptune	0.108351165×10^78	0.113015946×10^78
Pluto	0.087764443×10^78	0.0860632×10^78

APPENDIX Table; Kinetic energy at each apex bound Treo, in orbits of planets placed at its Planetary Quantum levels.

(G) Why are Waves formed

Have you ever thought why waves (EM, Matter, and gravitational) are formed? It is to support the matter in the Space matrix. Any EM energy or mass energy packet, or any mass at gravitational centre, or even diluted mass pressure of body presented as Load of body on its any layer e.g., from the Sun, will spread on its wave and will be supported at each apex bound Treo by its kinetic column.

Each quantum energy can only be supported by its one rotation on the matrix; (S free treos in one quanta energy is to be supported by S kinetons, with in S vibration when each kineton rotates in S directions of a circle). Any packet load will thus be supported on the matrix in a minimum period of S vibrations in one second.

For photons, transverse sub-kinetic columns at each apex bound Treo rotate and complete one full rotation for each quanta energy of a photon packet as one EM wave. Thus, it forms equal number of EM waves to support the total number of quanta EM energy in the packet in one second.

While in a mass energy packet, to support its load of 'Square number of Quanta of its quantum level number' at each apex bound Treo in its wavelength, requires equal number of orbitums in all sub-shells of shell.

All equal energy orbitums in any sub shell, one over the other placed in its vertical wave length, jointly form the structure of its one orbit.

To balance angular momentum in any atomic orbit, it's half of the orbitums in wave length, will rotate clockwise to lodge the + spin energetic electron, and the other half of the orbitums in the same orbit rotate anticlockwise to lodge the – spin electron.

Thus, the total number of EM waves or the total number of orbitums in all shells present at each apex bound Treo along the wavelength is always equal to the total number of quanta that form this packet and will be supported in one second (S vibrations).

Figure 10; shows matter waves at the first four quantum levels with decreasing numbers of shells in the vertically placed wave in its wavelength, with 1 orbitum in *S*, 3 orbitums in *p*, 5 orbitums in *d*, and 7 orbitums in *f* subshell. Out of all the orbitums in a wave, one over the other forms 1, 3, 5, 7 orbits.

Gravitational wave of any cosmic body in any orbit = formed by joining of number of matter waves which are equal to total 'unit masses' in body.

(!) COMMON FORMULA FOR LENGTH OF SPREAD OF ALL PACKETS.

Waves (electromagnetic, matter, and gravitational) form to support matter in the space matrix. For photons 'EM energy packet', transverse sub-kinetic columns rotate to support the energy packet, while 'mass energy packets' require shells with orbitums in sub shells forming vertical placed matter waves. Where each orbitum rotates once in one second and to balance angular momentum half of them rotates clockwise and half anti-clockwise to accommodate + spin electron and – spin electron in same orbit formed by total orbitums in wave length.

(!!) Formula for wavelength and frequency of wave:

Wavelength=S bound treos /divided by Number of quanta in the packet.

Where number of quanta in packet = Frequency of EM or matter wave.

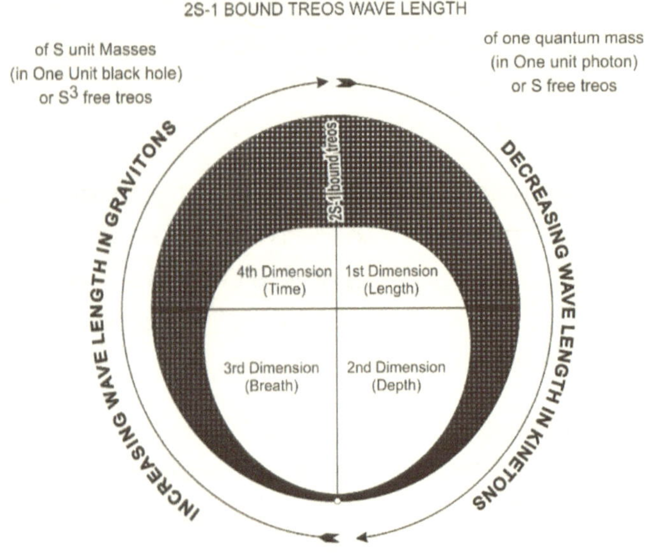

Increasing mass energy from one unit photon (S free treos mass energy) to one unit mass (S^2 free treos mass energy) **gradually contract** on successive **decreasing wave length** from 2S-1 bound treos to just one bound treo wave length (on one **graviton**) with the completion of deformation in first and second dimension.

Then increasing mass energy in unit of 'one unit mass' and its load in 'square of unit masses' at its gravitational center, '**spreads as 'diluted mass pressure'** (as 2n-1 unit masses in any direction) **in surrounding space matrix** on gradually **increasing wave length** as each successive bigger layer from one graviton of 'one unit mass' to 2S -1 gravitons of 'one unit black hole' (S unit masses) and thus form bigger gravitational fields with the completion of deformation in 3rd and 4th dimension.

Figure 23 – Wavelength reduces from S bound Treos of (unit photon) to just one of (unit mass) in the first and second dimension {@ = S number bound treos/ number of quanta energy in the packet (while frequency increases from 1 to 10^43)}. In the third and fourth dimension, wavelength increases from 1 To S bound Treos (while frequency decreases from 10^43 to 1).

(!!!) Calculations to verify, e.g., wave of an electron.

We will verify all the above statements with the example of the wavelength of a unit electron.

(A) <u>Reduced Compton (RC) wavelength</u> of 0.51 Mev unit Electron = 0.38615926796 × 10^-12 m (conventional value)

Or = 23.797258 × 10^21 Bound treos length (after conversion).

This can also be calculated by this new proposed formula: RC Wavelength of Electron = S bound Treo distance/quanta mass energy in electron packet.

23.797258 × 10^21 bound treos length = 1.855394419 10^43 bound Treo distance / 0.779667093 10^21 quanta electron.

(B) <u>Compton wavelength (circumference of Orbit)</u> of a 0.51 Mev electron is: = 2.42728683(11) × 10^-12 m [CO-DATA 2018 value]

Or = 1.50179695 × 10^23 bound Treo distance (after conversion).

The twice-reduced Compton wavelength, when multiplied by π, equals the circumference of an orbit or its Compton wavelength.

2 × 23.797258 × 10^21 bound treos length × π = 1.50179695 × 10^23 bound Treo length, which is the same as the CO-DATA value.

(C) The reduced Compton wavelength multiplied by the mass-energy of an electron (or any elementary particle) is the same as S^2 free treos,

as calculated = 23.797258 × 10^21 bound treos wavelength × 1.439491604 × 10^64 free treos in an electron packet = 3.4 × 10^86 = S^2 free treos (= S^2 kinetons as the ground energy of the second dimension).

<u>Inferences:</u> If the reduced Compton wavelength is **'n'**, then 2 × reduced Compton wavelength equals **2n-1** bound treos on which it forms one wave in an arc of 1/3rd circumference of a circle.

Furthermore, **2n-1 bound treos × π equals to the Compton wavelength, which is the circumference of its orbit.** (2n-1 is one layer of kinetic coloumn)

APPENDIX B

Science in the middle-ages and ancient India

(3) Understanding Gravitation

Bhaskaracharya or Bhaskar II (1114 CE – 1185 CE) wrote about gravitation and the motion of celestial bodies in his book "Shidhantasiromani" in the 12th century when he was 36 years old. He was the head of the astronomical observatory in Ujjain, India. But even before him, Brahmagupta (598 CE – 670 CE) discussed gravitation in the 7th century in his book "Brahmasphutasiddhanta" (originally written in 628 CE). It was reprinted in Banaras in 1902. Brahmagupta gave the name "Gurutwakarshan" (meaning "attraction by the big") to the concept, while Newton discovered it much later based on Kepler's studies in the 17th century.

(4) Legendary Figures

Aryabhata (476 AD – 550 AD), a student of Nalanda University, wrote "Arya Bhatiya" at the age of 23 in 499 AD. He also wrote "Arya-Siddhanta," and its third book only survives in its Arabic translation, known as "Al-Nanf." His work in mathematics includes (1) "Gatikapada," which consists of 13 verses and includes tables of sine (JYA), cosine (KOJYA), versine (UTKARAMA), and inverse sine (OTKRAM JYA), which influenced the birth of trigonometry. (2) "Ganitapada," which consists of 33 verses and covers arithmetic and geometric progression, GENOME shadows (Shanku chhaya), simple, quadratic, simultaneous, and indeterminate equations (Kuttaka). (3) "Kalakriyapada," which consists of 25 verses and describes periods of time and methods of determining the positions of planets, as well as the names of the seven days in a week. (4) "Golapada," which consists of 50 verses and explores the geometric and trigonometric aspects of the celestial sphere, including features of the ecliptic, celestial equator, nodes, causes of day and night, and the rising of zodiacal signs on the horizon

The work was influenced by LALLA, BHASKARA 1, BRAHMAGUPTA, and VARAHMIHIRA, among others. Famous commentaries on his work are BHASHYA (600 AD) by BHASKARA 1 and ARYABHATIYA BHASH (in 1465 AD) written by Neelkanth Swami Ji. LATA DEVI (505 AD) was an astronomer.

LATA DEVI, a student of Arya Bhatt, contributed to SURYA-SIDHANTA (400 AD to 500 AD). The original is a palm leaf manuscript that serves as the basis of JYOTISH and PAN-CHANG, which are still prevalent in Hindu society. It also influenced the Islamic JALALI CALENDAR (1073 CE) based on actual solar transits, with seasonal errors less than the GEORGIAN CALENDAR. The text *describes Earth as spherical*, discusses the motion of the sun and moon relative to different constellations, provides the *diameter of various planets, and describes the orbits of astronomical bodies.* LATA DEVI also gives *explanations of lunar eclipses, solar eclipses, the rotation of Earth on its axis, the tropical year* (time taken for one revolution of Earth), *the reflection of light by the moon's surface, sinusoidal functions, solutions to single-variable quadratic equations, the value of pi up to 4 decimals, the diameter of Earth as 8000 miles* (corrected to 7928), *the diameter of the moon as 2400 miles* (corrected to 2160), *the distance between Earth and the moon as 258000 miles* (which actually varies to a maximum of 252700 *miles), the calculation of the length of the sidereal year, and the inclusion of relativity in motion.* The text is known for the *earliest known descriptions of sexagesimal fractions and trigonometric functions.*

<u>SRINIVASA RAMANUJAN AIYANGAR, FRS (20th Dec 1887 – 26 April 1920)</u>, had no formal education in pure mathematics but made substantial contributions to MATHEMATICAL ANALYSIS, NUMBER THEORY, INFINITE SERIES, and CONTINUED FRACTIONS, including solutions to mathematical problems that were considered unsolvable at the time.

(5) Earthquake predictions in India

Earthquake prediction is discussed as one full chapter in BRIHAT SAMHITA, written by Rishi Varaha Mihira (505 AD – 587 AD) in the 6th century CE (Gupta period) in Ujjain, MP. It describes the changed pattern of clouds, abnormal behaviour of animals and birds, the effect of the position of planets, changes in groundwater level, and the strange appearance of multiple coloured "Earthquake clouds" forming 7 days before an earthquake. These clouds are formed due to "vertical electrical fields" generated.

(6) OLD EDUCATION CENTRES OF INDIA (Nalanda University and Taksha-Shila University)

Nalanda University the biggest advanced university in India was built in the 4th century. It covered an area of 10 km and was built by the Gupta dynasty. It served for 800 years and attracted students from all over the world, with the majority being from China, Japan, Afghanistan, and Korea. Nalanda University had 1500 teachers and 10,000 students studying 100 subjects, including medical science, Ayurvedic medicine, physics, astrology, and astronomy.

In AD 1190, a madman named Mohammad Bakhtiyar Khilji burned 900,000 handwritten books and palm leaf manuscripts kept in its library. The fire burned for 3 months, and the remains of the burnt university, which cover a 23-acre excavation site, serve as an archaeological site and evidence of this event. The university, now a UNESCO world heritage site, suffered a fate similar to the library of Alexandria, which also burned in 48 BC. Some of the manuscripts saved by fleeing scholars can be seen at the Yarlung Museum in Tibet and the Los Angeles County Museum of Art. Luckily, the university is now being revived. Xuanzang, the monk who brought Buddhism to the East, arrived in India after a 17-year journey, mostly under the cover of darkness, in 629 CE. In 645 CE, he carried 657 manuscripts from Nalanda and translated them into Chinese, spreading them along with one of his Japanese disciples, Dosho, who spread them in Japan, where Buddhism remains a major religion to this day.

Taksha-Shila University was the oldest university in the world, was also in undivided Indian. It offered teaching in 64 streams and was built around the 5th century BC. It was later abandoned in the 5th century CE. The university was located in the city of Taxila, which was built by King Bharat, the younger brother of Lord Ram, in the name of his son Taksh. In Sanskrit, the city is called Taksha-Shila. The city is situated on the banks of the Indus River, which is now located in the Rawalpindi-Islamabad metropolis in Pakistan after the partition of India.

GLOSSARY

(A) TREO, also named Strings, exists only in one dimension of Planck's least length.

(i) Bound treos (Dark energy particles which constitutes 67% universe)

They are precursor of five positive dimensions alternately interwoven with voids, to form ten dimensions of SPACE-TIME-ENERGY.

(ii) Free Treo (Visible matter, 5% universe)

One quantum EM energy is present in unit photon (S number of free treos), and $\sqrt{S}$ quanta mass energy ($\sqrt{S}$ x S free treos) constitutes unit electron. S quanta (S x S free treos) is in unit mass (PLANCK'S MASS or 2.172×10^{-8} Kg).

(iii) KINETONS (deformed bound Treos) or Dark matter particles which constitute 27% universe.

(B) VOID are curled up 5 negative dimensions of empty spaces which are slowly uncurling.

(C) Space-Matrix (Space-Time-Energy);

The omnipresent matrix of the universe is the chromodynamic energy of the functional god.

Out of its 3 interdependent components of Space matrix, when SPACE CONTRACTS (by the conversion of bound treos into kinetons), Kinetic ENERGY FIELD FORMS and kinetic energy Erupts, while TIME slows down.

Thus, the ACTION-REACTION mechanism is executed in universe.

(D) **COLUMN GEOMETRY (2n-1 units in each layer and n^2 in any n-layered coloumn)**

The units of the 5 dimensions are **kineton** (1 kineton), **orbitum** (S kinetons), **graviton** (S^2 kinetons), **electron black hole** (S^3 kinetons), and **unit black hole** (S^4 kinetons), respectively which accumulates as per coloumn geometry to form √S layered supporting kinetic coloumns of each dimension.

(E) **DIFFERENT SUPPORTING STRUCTURES: (Unit – layer – KINETIC COLUMN) in all five dimensions.**

(i) Kinetons – kineton layers-and SUB KINETIC COLOUMN (simile – as if 1 knot in omnipresent mosquito net)

(ii) Orbitum-subshells – and SHELLS (1 & 2 Knots)

(iii) Graviton – spiral layers – ELECTRON BLACK HOLE (1, 2, and 3 Knots)

(iV) Electron black hole – Graviton layers of gravitational sphere – and GRAVITATIONAL SPHERE (1, 2, 3, and 4 Knots)

(V) Unit black hole-galactic centres – ultra massive black hole and biggest is KSHIR SAGAR. (1, 2, 3, 4, and 5 Knots one over the other; like Russian dolls)

(F) Some **VEDIC NAMES USED IN THE BOOK**

(1) BRAHMA – GOD OF CREATION

(2) SAD-BRAHMA (primordial soup) was converted to ASAD-BRAHMA (Space-Time-Energy: SPACE MATRIX)

(3) VISHNU (point A) – GOD OF CHROMODYNAMIC ENERGY OF UNIVERSE: as the gravitational centre of S^3 gravitons around the

centre of Kshir Sagar supports the load of S black holes (load of √S unit black holes mass).

(4) SHIV as Voids – GOD OF DESTRUCTION

Three Hindu G O D – G (generator; BRAHMA): O (operator; VISHNU): D (destructor; SHIV)

Likewise, BHAGVAN pronounced for God in Hindi, means BH (BHumi in Hindi means Earth) G (Gagan or Space) V (Vayu or Air) A (Agni or FIRE) N (Neer or Water); all five are, as *Earth, Space, Air, Fire and Water* which makes our body.

(5) RUDRA – Black hole

(6) KSHIR SAGAR – ultra-massive √S unit black holes

(7) INDRA – (KA particle) – King of all Dev (elements): Name given to 'MASS UNIT' of 35.01 MeV its integral multiples generate all visible matter.

(8) GANESH – (name given to 'unit electron')

(9) SAT-VRNDARAKAHA – Six Quarks

(10) TRI-VATRAMA – 3 Mesons

(11) ARYAMA – Uranus

(12) VARUN – Neptune

(13) RITU – Pluto

(14) SATURN RINGS – in Veda they are named as Shukra, Suchaya, and Rucha Naha.

(15) GURU-TWA-KARSHAN (attraction of BIG) – name given to Gravity (in book 'braham-sphot-shidhant,' original 628 CE)

BIBLIOGRAPHY

1. Ashok Saxena et al. Load Dependent Increase of Space-Time-Energy Contraction, Generating Four Forces and leading to Quantum Gravity. 2021; http://vixra.org/abs/2108.0046v1

2. Ashok Saxena et al, Treo model, Structure and working of the universe; Space matrix, Fifth Dimension & cosmic code. 2020; http://vixra.org/abs/2012.0165?Ref=12084892

3. Ashok Saxena et al, Treo model, Structure and working of the universe; unification of forces and quantum gravitation. 2020; http://vixra.org/abs/2012.0167?Ref=12084909

4. Ashok Saxena et al, Treo model, Structure and working of the universe; Increasing deformation of unit space matrix and formation of all elements. 2020; http://vixra.org/abs/2012.0171?Ref=11808447

5. Ashok Saxena et al. Position of Baby bodies in any gravitational field, 2020; http://vixra.org/abs/2011.0097?Ref=12084860

6. Ashok Saxena et al. Confirmation of Treo model even outside the solar system. 2020; http://vixra.org/abs/2011.0096?Ref=12084878

7. Ashok Saxena et al. Formation of energetic charged particles in Lower Magnetosphere and their sporadic showers through the ecliptic window, explaining all total solar eclipse-related phenomena. 2021; http://vixra.org/abs/2108.0047v1

8. Ashok Saxena; Treo Model of Structure and Working of Universe (Cosmic code), (INDIA) ISBN 978-1-64828-887-6

paperback, Notion press, e-book ISBN 978-1-64828888-3 (Notion press). 2020; Copyright number, L 94591/2020; https://archive.org/details/treo-model-of-structure-and-working-of-universe-cosmic-code

9. Ashok Saxena. Our universe and how it works; (Quantum gravitation and Fifth dimension), (India) hard copy ISBN 978-93-5235-003-2 (Manas Prakashan); 2015, and 2016 e-book, ISBN 978-93-5235-065-0, Book baby. https://ia601509.us.archive.org/0/items/our-universe-and-how-it-works-1/Our%20universe%20and%20how%20it%20works%20%20%20%281%29.pdf

10. Ashok Saxena. Inside a Wave, paperback book (India), Manas Prakashan, 2005, (Book Copyright no. L-36882/2010/19-11-2010).

11. Ashok, Ashwarya, Amit Saxena. Quantum gravity and its preponed birth (INDIA)

    ISBN-978-8-89002-981-2, Notion press; 2023, e book.

    https://books.google.com.sg/books?id=UjrCEAAAQBAJ

12. Ashok Saxena, Matter, Dark Matter, and Dark Energy in the perspective of the New Theory of Quantum Gravitation. 2021; http://vixra.org/abs/2111.0046

13. Dr. K. C. Sharma, Modern atomic structure as described in the Vedas, 1996, ISBN 978-81-7325-834-1

14. Ashok Saxena, Srivastava K P; "Electrical stimulation in delayed union of long bones." Acta Orthopaedica Scandinavia, Vol. 48, pages 561-565, 1977

15. Ashok Saxena, Srivastava K P, Srivastava P K; "Potentiometric studies in the case of delayed union of long bones treated by electrical stimulation." Indian Journal of Orthopaedics, Vol. 12, No. 1, pages 25-32, 1978.

16. Ashok Saxena, Srivastava K P; "Electrical stimulation in cases of delayed union of long bones." 196-197, YEARBOOK OF ORTHOPAEDICS, 1979.

ACKNOWLEDGMENTS

First and foremost, I extend my deepest gratitude to the divine power that guided and inspired me to undertake this work. I also wish to thank my late wife, Prof. Dr. Surekha Saxena, whose unwavering support and editorial assistance were invaluable throughout this journey.

My heartfelt thanks go to my son, Er. Amit Saxena, for his dedication in compiling this book, and to Er. S. K. Bhandari, who generously provided all the necessary literature related to the Vedas.

I am also deeply grateful to my mentor, Dr. R.C. Saxena, who served as the peer reviewer for all my work. I would like to extend my appreciation to the other peer reviewers: Mr. Avinash Mathur, the late Prof. H. P. Sinha, Dr. Anurag Saxena, Er Ashwarya Saxena and Dr. Gita Madhu for their insightful contributions.

Lastly, I hope that this work serves humanity by offering knowledge with extraordinary discussion with alien which can change the course of all sciences, with this engaging exploration of the nature of creation and its wonders.

www.ingramcontent.com/pod-product-compliance
Lightning Source LLC
Chambersburg PA
CBHW031628170726
47990CB00017B/407